The Urbana Free Library

To renew: call 217-367-4057
or go to "*urbanafreelibrary.org*"
and select "Renew/Request Items"

KIRILL KOBRIN

ELEVEN PRAGUE CORPSES

STORIES

Translated by Veronika Lakotová

DALKEY ARCHIVE PRESS

© 2016 by Kirill Kobrin
Translation © 2016 by Veronika Lakotová
First edition, 2016

Library of Congress Cataloging-in-Publication Data

Names: Kobrin, Kirill, 1964- author. | Lakotová, Veronika, translator.
Title: Eleven Prague corpses / by Kirill Kobrin ; translated by Veronika
    Lakotová.
Other titles: 11 Prague corpses
Description: Victoria, TX : Dalkey Archive Press, 2016. | Collection of
    stories that appeared in various Russian magazines and also online.
Identifiers: LCCN 2015040719 | ISBN 9781628971347 (pbk. : alk.
paper)
Classification: LCC PG3482.6.O37 A2 2016 | DDC 891.73/5--dc23
LC record available at http://lccn.loc.gov/2015040719

The publication was effected under the auspices of the
Mikhail Prokhorov Foundation TRANSCRIPT Pro-
gramme to Support Translations of Russian Literature.

  transcript

Partially funded by the Illinois Arts Council, a state agency.

Dalkey Archive Press publications are, in part, made possible through the
support of the University of Houston-Victoria and its programs in
creative writing, publishing, and translation.

Dalkey Archive Press
Victoria, TX / McLean, IL / Dublin / London
www.dalkeyarchive.com

Typesetting: Mikhail Iliatov
Printed on permanent/durable acid-free paper

Contents

Eleven Prague Corpses

The Final Line

Maurice approached me at the funeral. He said—stuttering as usual and as usual, in broken English—"An appropriate way of dying for a former restaurant critic, isn't it? Professional, so to speak. Acute pancreatitis. Caused by what? By the exceptional Czech dumplings, pork, and beer. And of course, by the always exceptional Czech doctors. Damned Prague." It started to drizzle, the heavy scent of the earth mixed with the smell of damp clothes. It was difficult to breathe. "Damned Prague," I agreed. "Damned Central Europe." Maurice merrily continued: "Damned life. Poor Jean. He kicked the bucket in a hospital whose name he couldn't even pronounce . . . I can't, either. How is it—Karč? Kyrč?" "Krč." "Well Peter, you're Russian and Slavic, and a barbarian, you can make a growl and a hiss at the same time but we, the refined French, can't twist our delicate tongues enough to make those cave-like sounds. And some of us find their last cave here . . ." "Maurice, give them some credit, it wasn't Slavic sounds at all that caused Jean's death, it was . . ." "Yes, yes, barbarian food and barbarian health care. Poor Jean, just imagine, only ten years ago the best restaurateurs of the *belle France* trembled at the mere sound of his name." Maurice's Frenchified English was unbearable. And so was my Russified English. On the whole, my English made my life in Prague unbearable—possibly even more so than my poor knowledge of Czech. And to top it all off, going back and forth between the universal vernacular and the provincial dialect was rotting my mother tongue, and my character was rotting along with it. I actually thought up a name for this disease—"the Prague syndrome"—and strove to cure like with like, avoiding both the natives and the local Russians. As a result of this I became a regular of expat bars and English-language bookshops, where I swilled down my evenings together with thin beer and down-and-out conversations in *lingua angla*. It was in one of those bars a year and a half before when I first met Jean.

One of the numerous misconceptions in my life (most of which I'd developed in my childhood from books such as *The Three Muske-*

teers) was that the French scorned beer. Nonsense. The French adore beer, at least Jean adored beer, while not neglecting wine. And he couldn't neglect it, since drinking it was his professional duty, especially, as he used to say, in the old and better days in his homeland. How one of the leading Parisian restaurant critics had turned into a culinary observer of an ordinary English-language magazine in an ordinary capital city of an ordinary former province of the Austro-Hungarian Empire, Jean never explained, nor did I ask. We used to sit in Shakespeare and Sons sipping Bernard beer (dark in the winter, light in the summer), and exchanged opinions on music. Never on food. Never. From time to time Jean would recommend a newly opened Middle Eastern joint that served nice meals but he'd never express enthusiasm about the quality of its hummus or couscous. He sounded disinterested even in his column in the *Prague Herald*. He praised restaurants only when their owners requested him to, and happily took their money for it. No one knew about his distinguished Parisian past, myself included—until Maurice showed up in Prague.

Maurice had moved to Prague several months before and already a week later he became a fixture in Shakespeare and Sons. He'd opened a small herbal shop in the Vinohrady district of Prague and planned to get rich quickly, inviting the Czech clerks with impossibly short haircuts and their solarium-fried girlfriends into his Eastern herbal paradise. It became clear quite soon that, apart from two or three bored elderly Swedish women who'd bought apartments in the recently renovated house nearby, nobody ever came to his shop. The local middle class was busy stuffing itself with cholesterol, beer, and antibiotics just like before, showing no interest in the spirit-lifting selections of Vedic herbs or a miraculous oil from the bark of an Australian bush. Behind the counter Maurice placed a frightful-looking Indian woman, a former waitress in the restaurant Taj Mahal, and he did quite little: by day, he visited secondhand bookshops and junk dealers, dreaming of discovering an unknown Kafka manuscript that he could sell and thereby make up for his homeopathics fiasco. In the evenings, he sat around with us in Shakespeare's, ruthlessly complaining about the Czechs. Once, when Jean was again in the hospital for observation—he had heart problems—Maurice, alone with me at a table in Shakespeare's, told me the story of how the successful restaurant critic had ruined his career.

This was how he described it. Jean secretly visited restaurants that had the Michelin stars of excellence, checking the relation between the high award and the reality. As his face was so well-known, he used wigs, false beards and moustaches, and once he even pretended to be an Indian, his head wrapped up in a turban. After the masquerade came the retaliation. Jean showed no mercy in the face of obtrusive sauces, half-withered vegetable tips, and the imperfections of both napkins and waiters. When he praised, he did so reluctantly and as if through gritted teeth. He especially criticized the apostles of the "nouvelle cuisine," the warriors against calories, the knights of raw-foodism. Jean called them "herbivores" and accused them of all mortal sins, ranging from charlatanism to forgetting the ancient traditions of the fine French cooking. Liberal society was inflamed, the rightists were applauding, and peasants, opposed to globalization, sent him several wheels of intoxicatingly fat and intoxicatingly strong cheese as a present of gratitude. Maurice believed Jean had deliberately played the role of an iconoclast in a society addicted to fitness and multiculturalism. As to whether this was sincere and in earnest, Maurice didn't know. At any rate, the whole thing took a completely different turn after Jean visited Savarin, an outstanding restaurant in a Parisian suburb. The facility, crowned with Michelin stars, was run by one of the most fashionable chefs of the nineties, Christophe Frezze. He was an elderly gentleman who'd come a long and surprising way from a cook in an Italian tavern in Nice to the ownership of the restaurant where in the evening you could meet, for instance, a former president of the country—a famous gourmand—or a famed long-nosed English novelist and culinary writer, crazy about everything French from the Norman Flaubert to the Lorrainian foie gras. Jean dedicated nine-tenths of the respective text of his "Travels to the Edge of the Plate" to the raptures about the delicacy and lightness of the Savarin meals. He composed a eulogy about crayfish tails with truffles and vegetable balls, confessed his romantic feelings for the Bresse chicken with morel mushrooms, acknowledged the undoubted qualities of Riesling "Clos Sainte Hune" (F. E. Trimbach, 1983), remarked on the courtesy and experience of the waiters, dedicated a few sentences to an appreciative analysis of the restaurant design, and even granted moderate praise to the menu's typeface. However, the last paragraph, in Maurice's words, dealt the fatal blow. It started with the sentence: "I left Savarin, as it is required nowadays, feeling slightly hungry." Further on the critic asked: "So what was it for that I paid the sum equal to the week's salary of a teacher?" and went on in the vein that we should be going to restaurants in order to eat and—he made a strong point of this—to *fill ourselves up*. Next, Jean came down on contemporary society with its fear of, as he put it, "simple human joys," for example "to stuff one's belly with delicious food." A Spenglerian conclusion followed: "Our civilization is doomed. Almost doomed. In order to save it, we have to eat well and much. Mountains of stewed and roasted meat together with fried potatoes are our barricades; long baguettes with crunchy crust are our lances. The good old local wine will make our colorless blood crimson again. Such restaurants as Savarin are the enemies' headquarters in our culinary territory and Christophe Frezze—albeit half-Italian—is a traitor to French traditions. Next time I want to eat, that is *to eat*, and not to spend a pile of money, instead of Savarin I shall head for McDonald's." The morning after his column "Travels to the Edge of the Plate" appeared, Christophe Frezze committed suicide.

Everyone fell upon Jean—both his enemies and his former allies. His column was closed down, he was fired from the newspaper, other periodicals refused to take any articles signed with his name. Hoping to wait out the storm, Jean left for Ireland for a few weeks, but when he came back, the scandal was still in full swing. "Villain," "dangerous loudmouth," "cuisine churl" were the softest characteristics that restaurant owners, journalists, politicians, and philosophizing shepherds of the public opinion used regarding his person.

Somehow there appeared that long-nosed Englishman in the

street: he came up to Jean and gave him a slap in the face, and nearby bushes lit up with camera flashes. The following day newspapers extensively reported on the incident and it seemed that for the first time in history, everyone in Paris took the side of an Englishman. There was even talk of legal proceedings but the late Frezze had no close kin: he'd divorced his first wife long before; he hadn't seen his son from that marriage for many years and never started a new family. There were rumors that the son would be found at any moment, but Jean didn't tempt fate and escaped to the east—first to Germany, but after the importunate journalists discovered him there, he set out further and settled in Prague. Here, he returned to working as a food critic with a pseudonym but of course, it wasn't the same Jean anymore. Moreover, the disaster had left—in the literal sense of the word—scars on his heart. This circumstance played a crucial role in his life and also in his death, but more about that later. Maurice didn't answer the most important question anyway—whether Jean suffered any remorse as a result of Christophe Frezze's suicide.

The day after Jean's burial, I read his obituary in the new issue of the *Prague Herald*. Its author paid due tribute to the qualities of the deceased but the overall tone was restrained. "A famous restaurant critic," "tireless explorer of new islands of true cuisine," "an important member of the Prague expats' society," "tragic, hideous death." Well, only the necessary stuff. No need to go on about Jean's Parisian escapades or about how he bungled his work in the Prague magazine, about that atrocious personality of his that had frightened away all his acquaintances in Prague in such a way that he ended up spending evenings in the company of a local Russian historian and his own homeopathic fellow countryman brought here by God knows what! But if anything in the obit was true to fact, it was the words about his hideous and tragic death. Jean died in a stupid way, somehow in a special Prague way, in a Central European way. He didn't come to Shakespeare's for several evenings in a row and when I called him to find out what had happened, Jean referred to doctors who'd prescribed for him a three-day abstinence. "And not only from beer," he concluded cryptically. In the morning Jean texted me, suggesting that we meet in the evening at our usual place. During the day he was to visit a newly opened spot, specially designed for German and British tourists; its name was "Czech Standard" and it welcomed foreigners with frightening local exotica—heaps of fat pork, fortified walls of boiled dough bathing in thick brown lakes of meat gravy, and barrels of Pilsner. I remember that morning I felt sorry for Jean, who had to experience all that at once, in a single visit. In the evening he again failed to appear in Shakespeare's. Next morning Maurice called me and said that Jean had been brought to the hospital with a heart attack and within twenty-four hours, when we set out to visit him in that vowelless Krč, he was already dead. The doctors had made a little mistake—they jabbed heart medications into him while his pancreas was literally soaked with the surplus of fat and rich food. Intending to improve blood circulation, they gave him blood-thinning substances at the same time that his stomach was flooded with blood. Too late did they notice the peritonitis. Maurice told me that Jean, while he could still talk, attempted to explain something to the doctors and nurses, but they couldn't speak either French or English and advised him to speak in Czech, as being in the Czech Republic, he was supposed to communicate in the corresponding language. Obviously, he wanted to disclose something to them about his condition that could've shown them the right way, but ... There was no sense in bringing legal action against the hospital and there was no one to do so; at least I wasn't planning to undergo legal proceedings in Kafka's homeland. So, that was the end of it. Jean was irrevocably dead and the ecstatic review on the Czech Standard was written up by a *Herald* intern. "As if you glanced into the belly of the good old Bohemia!" was the conclusion to his excellent article.

I received a phone call from Jean's landlady a week after the funeral. That strange creature was capable of never being where she should be when the tenants needed her—first I, and then Jean, to whom I'd left my apartment when I could no longer afford it. Jana, regardless of her age of sixty-something, armed herself with that something and used to disappear into the Czech spa towns, spinning highland affairs with the local elderly Don Juans, and always had her cell phone conveniently switched off. Now too, she found on her return from the Krkonoše Mountains that her tenant had been dead for eight days. No one came to take away his belongings, and meanwhile the apartment lay empty and wasn't bringing income sufficient for playing around in the Krkonoše. Jana begged me with a tear in her eye — in the name of our old friendship — to clear the apartment of the deceased man's belongings. I refused for a long time, referring to the illegality of such an action, a possible appearance of heirs, etc., but when the tears wetted the landlady's voice, I gave up. After work I had a quick lunch in a Chinese joint, hidden in a dirty passageway that twisted from the crowded Wenceslas Square, and then went up the square, towards the gigantic building of the Museum of Natural History, walked through a tiny park, making a point of not looking sideways at the heroin-destroyed shabby youth, turned right, bravely marched past a music shop where they'd just put up a new Paolo Conte album in the window, then straight, without stopping, till the end of that endless street, to the point where the tram makes a sharp turn downwards. It was there that my former house stood. And Jean's former house as well.

There were few things. I agreed to take with me the collection of CDs, a few books; as for the clothes, I advised her to take them to a charity shop and suggested that she keep the player herself — as a compensation of the emotional damage arising from the premature death of her beloved tenant. All the furniture belonged to her, so all she had to do was to wash the floor, throw out the empty little colorful boxes from some mysterious medicines that had failed to save Jean's life, to dust the place, and to look for a new — and healthier — tenant. Just before I went out the door, I remembered Maurice and took for him one of the items of pottery that remained after our friend. I chose a large English mug from the Selfridges collection.

I knew all Jean's CDs by heart, and at home I arranged them together with my music in a different, but fully natural order: Shostakovich with Shostakovich, Glass with Glass, Piazzolla with Piazzolla, Paris Combo with Rachid Taha, Ute Lemper, and Iva Bittová.

Jean was all right when it came to music; music was the only thing we ever talked about because everything else was a cause for him to get offended by and raise hell about. On the whole, it wasn't clear at all why I spent evenings in his company, though, with whom can a Russian spend his evenings in Prague, if he fears his fellow countrymen like the plague—the old and the new ones alike? I've got few acquaintances; as for friends—none at all. Dusty sheets of paper in the Jesuit archive by day, my usual company in the evenings, sometimes a beer in Shakespeare's, the latest edition of the *Guardian*, a familiar detective novel for bedtime reading. On Saturday—lunch with Vlasta and spending time together. On Sunday—burying myself in Derzhavin or Vyazemsky, going for a walk, turning in earlier than usual. That's it. And that was about the rhythm Jean had here, only he, instead of archive dust, daily swallowed the dubious masterpieces of Prague chefs . . . His books had been randomly chosen—*Les Enfants Terribles* by Cocteau neighboring Chinese fairytales, *Story of O* next to a most boring work of Braudel's, *The Identity of France*. Among them I discovered something which at first I took for a book—it boasted a saffian cover and expensive yellow paper. It was a journal. Turning it over for a moment, I decided that there was now nobody to be offended, except for God, but he doesn't exist and that means everything's permitted, and therefore I opened the first pages. As they wrote of yore, the confession of his soul was so disgusting that it was impossible not to immerse oneself in it.

Of course I fell on the comments related to that fateful visit of Savarin. They were surprisingly dry. "Sep 20. Been to Savarin. Best restaurant of recent years." "Sep 28. Be provocative?!" "Sep 29. Thought for a long time and then decided. My readers vote for Le Pen." "Sep 30. An excellent piece of writing, not worse than the Frezze chicken." "Oct 2. Frezze committed suicide." And so on, in the same telegraphic style, until his escape from Paris. The closer to Prague, the less attentively I read through the comments, and my mind was occupied with an important question—is it worth reading what that outcast wrote about me? Now and then, there appeared some vague threats that Jean received from unknown people, but I decided that first, this was already paranoia and second, I wouldn't read the comments on myself. I closed the journal, and set out to the Vinohrady — to give Maurice the Selfridges mug.

Maurice was sitting in his herbal shop and indifferently sorting the colorful little boxes containing the medicines. The Indian was compiling a report. Before I could ask anything, Maurice energetically slapped his neck with his hand and growled: "Enough, enough, enough! That's it! Enough. *Finita la commedia.* The shop's closing down. My Swedish ladies will be left without herbal tea and antiseptic dried flowers. If you see them, tell them this — may they stuff themselves with antibiotics. By kilograms! By tons! I'm leaving for the South Tyrol the day after tomorrow — I've been offered a position of a homeopath in a sanatorium. Never, you hear me; *never* shall I return to this backwater! By the way — I invite you to the Czech Standard tomorrow for a goodbye lunch. We'll eat enough dumplings to last us for the rest of our lives."

"What's this now?"

"What's what? My lease is up next week. They say there's going to be a furniture shop here. And as for the herbs . . . They're worth nothing. Well, almost nothing. I've told Lakshmi to take as much as she wants. By the way, do you need some? There's a lot here. You complained about your appetite, didn't you? Take this mixture, drink half a cup three times a day and no one will be able to drag you away from the dining table! Don't forget to drink it the day after tomorrow or you'll meet the same destiny as poor Jean!"

"Oh, yes, Jean. I've got a gift for you from the Other Side." I gave Maurice the mug and told him about the journal. "What, did he really write this — not worse than the Frezze chicken? Great! Well, our Jean, he was a real beast, and yet, I'm sorry for his stupid death. He didn't have to come here. He would've been much better off if he'd gone to the States or somewhere like Argentina. And what did he write about the two of us?"

"I didn't read that. Didn't want to get upset. I've put the notebook out of sight for a couple of months. I'll have a look later."

"Good for you! Otherwise we might hang ourselves just like old

Frezze, eh?"

"Hardly. And, Maurice, did Frezze actually hang himself? I never got around to asking what it was that he'd done . . ."

"Nothing was announced officially but there were rumors that he hanged himself on a hook in the hall, pinning a note to his chest . . ."

"Accusing Jean?"

"You're wrong. It read—'Feeling slightly hungry.'"

"Witty."

"Yes! So you didn't read his journal to the end?"

"No, I didn't. And I won't in the near future."

"Yes, indeed, you get to read a lot of interesting stuff every day, by your Jesuit fathers. I guess they're funny guys too . . ."

The following day I felt it was extremely kind of Maurice to deprive the Prague citizens of his medicines' healing powers. After two half-cups of the mixture, not only my appetite was gone—so was my will to live. My heart beat irregularly and weakly, my glasses were running with sweat, and the doctor I went to see after work gave me some heart-strengthening injection. I told him about the herbal tea; he shrugged his shoulders and stated his opinion that people should cure themselves with normal pills and not with charlatan powders and oils. At home I examined again the boxes I'd inherited from Maurice—no, everything was correct, I'd boiled and drunk just like the directions said I should. Towards the evening I got better and the next day, as if nothing had happened, I was sitting in the Czech Standard and cursing his homeopathy.

"I suppose you cured Jean with your poison as well. I saw some packets with familiar green leaves on the label at his place . . . Admit it Maurice, it was you who sent him to his grave, wasn't it?"

"Peter, I'm sorry, Lakshmi must've been in a rush when she was putting the bags from the case into the boxes and probably mistook intestinal herbs for those for the heart. Don't be angry, c'mon, you simply drank a potion for cardiacs who suffer from high blood pressure . . ."

"And now there's some poor bastard with three heart attacks in his medical history being pulled by his ears away from a Wiener Schnitzel?"

"No, don't imagine that. I threw in the garbage everything you and Lakshmi didn't take away."

"How generous of you, Maurice!"

"Let my generosity buy you a scotch!"

"I won't refuse. I only have to make sure they haven't swapped it for castor oil by mistake."

Then the Prague winter came, fog crept out from the cellars of the Old Town, dark Bernard beer took the place of the light one, a nice Polish lady started frequenting Shakespeare's, my linguistic experience got enriched with Polish-English and my sexual experience with Polish threesome. After New Year I decided to move in with Julita, and while packing my books, I came across Jean's journal among the things I use for my work with documents. I asked myself: should I take it? or not? or throw it away? or keep it in memory of him? what did he write there about me? Undecided, I opened the notebook at the end and discovered the absence of the last page. A less-experienced scholar would've said that there'd never been a page, but I — after many years' labor over Jesuit reports — am not to be deceived; there had been a page and it had been torn out. It was proved by tiny pieces of paper in the binding and the absence of the opposite page in the first half of the notebook. I put aside the cardboard box containing my books and reached for a magnifying glass and a special little lamp. And yes. The last comment in Jean's journal was indented on the following — empty — page. After half an hour's effort, I read it. There it stood: "Nov 6. Horrible Czech Standard. Horrible. But now I'm full."

My Polish girlfriend's apartment — thanks to her employer's generosity — amazed me with its size. I was assigned a spacious corner in which I could restore the workplace atmosphere of my own tiny place. While Julita was spoiling her shapely body in scented foam for hours on end, I leafed through that damned little notebook and brooded over the absent page. Basically, there were two questions. Is there any other meaning, apart from the obvious one, in the sentence, "Now I'm full"? Who tore out the final page and why? Strange as it may seem, to answer the second question—after I gave it some thought—was relatively easy. It was somebody else, not Jean, because that very night he was taken away by ambulance. Hardly would he, suffering from terrible pain, remember his journal. The more so because Jean obviously underestimated the Kafkaesque quality of Czech health care and didn't plan on leaving his apartment forever. It means that somebody went to the apartment while its tenant was parting with life in the Krč hospital. Doors are hard to break in these old houses and our landlady, although she roamed about the mountains, always closed the door firmly behind herself and the tenants. When I'd been living in that apartment, I had so many keys that it was difficult to fit the bunch in my pocket. That means whoever tore out the page, must have had the key. And there was only one way to get that key. All these reflections made me feel rather weird and I tried to look at it differently. Why would it be necessary to tear the page out from the journal? Whom could it disgrace? Certainly not the owners of Czech Standard, who'd never know their food had killed a restaurant critic . . . Of course not. The more so because the sentence I read, the last that Jean had written in his life, reminded me of something, but I couldn't for the life of me put my finger on it. It somehow resembled a line in a dialogue, the previous line of which I knew. And of course, the page was torn out by the person to whom the sentence was addressed, maybe in a symbolic way rather than straightforwardly—but still, addressed. And suddenly I realized whose that previous line was and who— instead of its author—pocketed Jean's dying reply. I got to see the truth of what had happened. It was so clear. Details alone remained that, within several days, I clarified with the help of the internet. My grandmother—a professor of medicine—would've been proud of me.

Then I decided to relate everything to Maurice—who else? He hadn't given me his new address but it was quite easy to discover the online coordinates of the Monte Magico sanatorium. It was even easier to find the products, as well as the email address of the sanatorium's homeopathic pharmacy. All that was left was to compose a letter, and that I did.

Dear Maurice!

Excuse my writing to your pharmacy address, as I don't know your private one and my letter will be partly dedicated to matters of health care and homeopathy. I've decided to remind you of a half-forgotten Prague story—undoubtedly in order to forget it forever and thus cure myself of certain memories. Time is, after all, a doctor more effective than your herbal pills and potions, isn't it? (One thing I'll never forget is your medication for improving the appetite! Pardon my impertinency, I will now fall silent about that incident . . .) I've recently spent a good number of hours leafing through the journal of our late friend Jean and contemplating the circumstances of his lamentable death. How was it possible to die in such a stupid way—to fill oneself up on Czech "food"? Why did he plunge after that roasted pork joint, those bread dumplings, that monstrous goulash, and one tankard of Pilsner after another? Isn't it weird, dear Maurice, taking into account that he'd never been fond of this "food" with the possible exception of beer? How did such a beastly and fateful appetite arise that day? You know, Maurice, after reading the penultimate comments in Jean's diary, I can answer this question. The thing is that a week before Jean's death, some doctor prescribed that he fast for three days, and so our starved restaurant critic gorged himself on this pitiful food. And that, dear Maurice, isn't everything. The same doctor prescribed that he—don't laugh, it's not a joke!—drink an herbal mixture to strengthen his heart, the one which I wound up drinking. Oh yes, it wasn't drunk by Jean but by myself, and our poor friend, starving, was taking an appetite-boosting medication for three days— the one which your humble servant was supposed to drink! Honestly, I took the pains to check the labels—of course, not those on the boxes that were lying around in Jean's apartment (those had been swept out by the unmerciful hand of our mountain-loving landlady), but I read the labels on the boxes that by chance found themselves at my place. So Maurice, your professional reputation is fully restored—it was me who fell victim to the accident that had swapped one medicine for another. That is—the accident that slipped the swapped medicine to your table and then—to me. By the way, this "accident" is most interesting. If there's anyone else to blame for Jean's death, apart from, of course, the Krč doctors, it is the "accident." It was this very accident that increased the hunger of our dear haute cuisine connoisseur so that he stuffed himself and died. Sad as it is, it's true.

In recent weeks I have very much wanted to talk to the doctor who—apart from curing the diseased heart of our friend by means of fasting—in such a fatal way mistook medicines which he'd labeled with his own hand. And finally, I've managed to do so. I'm talking to you, Maurice, although via Gmail. Wasn't it you who advised Jean full abstinence from food when he, holding his chest, staggered into your homeopathic shop? And you who slipped him—instead of a soothing mixture—something for improving the appetite? And it wasn't the first time that he'd turned to you for medical advice, was it? And of course, the most important question—didn't you know that he was about to go to the fearful Czech Standard and not to, say, a fashionable, expensive restaurant that you leave feeling slightly hungry? Yes, yes, yes, and yes. With a soft homeopathic touch, you forced our unsuspecting Jean to stuff his stomach full of simple peasant food and to die in horrible pain. You're right, Maurice, he paid the full price for his excellent sentence, "I left Savarin, as it is required nowadays, feeling slightly hungry." Jean finally *filled himself up*.

In the end when he got sick, very sick, he began to guess something vaguely and wrote down in his journal: "But now I'm full." While Jean was still in his senses, he managed to utter the final line in the dialogue with the late Christophe Frezze. Now this exchange of lines can be reconstructed in the following way:

Jean: I left Savarin, as it is required nowadays, feeling slightly hungry . . . Our civilization is doomed. Almost doomed. In order to save it, we have to eat well and much. Mountains of stewed and roasted meat together with fried potatoes are our barricades . . . Next time I want to eat, that is to *eat*, and not to spend a pile of money, instead of Savarin I shall head for McDonald's.

Christophe (hanging himself): Feeling slightly hungry.

Jean (dying of overeating): But now I'm full.

Well, Maurice, thanks to you the play has received an ideal conclusion. I'm not talking about the fact that you buried the cynical advocate of the "good old cuisine" by making use of good old "mountains of stewed and roasted meat," but you did so with the help of the contemporary culture of fasting and homeopathy, which he hated. Bravo! Christophe Frezze—was he really your father?—is revenged. I imagine the journal's last page, stolen by you, is framed and adorns the wall of your office. To be sure, this document is worth ten medical certificates.

On that, I part with you and wish you all the very best. If you can find the time, send me a note about your Tyrolean life (only, if possible, without medical advice!).

Yours,
Peter K.

P. S.: And the key, he gave it to you in the hospital? Probably asked you to bring him his gown and toothbrush?

Two weeks after this epistle (which remained unanswered), I received a registered letter with no return address. Inside the envelope, within diploma-like covers that had been handed out to the participants of the Annual World Conference of Homeopaths (Zürich, May 12–14, 2010), lay a sheet of fine yellow paper, embellished with a short inscription. I put back the missing page from where it had been torn and went on with my life.

The Triumph of Evil

I had three days left to submit the piece, so I didn't hurry. I pronounced the deceased man's last name, tapped the base of my front teeth with the tip of my tongue, inserted my tongue between the rows of teeth and then whistled. Mr. "Lengthy." Transliterated as *Lengfi*? Or *Lengsi*? Or, translated into Russian—*Dlinniy*? *Vysokiy*? *Ewan Vysokiy*. Funny. According to what I was sent by his inconsolable colleagues and staff, the deceased was short, which "didn't prevent him from taking an active part in the traditional football matches of our school: teachers vs. students." On my screen, I scrolled down through the text of the obit-writing endeavors of the staff at the Private British School in Prague. A very detailed draft. Too detailed. Why all that "attentive look of his blue eyes" stuff? Why "the kind smile always playing on the lips of our teacher and headmaster"? Why the "scar on his neck, received in the ranks of the Royal Marine Corps, fighting in the Falklands"? Sure, a hero of all possible wars starting with the Korean War. I'll dump it all, of course. After all, I've been writing obituaries for the *Prague Herald* these past two years. I've become rather proficient in this genre from the time I sweated out my very first last-goodbye for a poor Frenchman who carried out his duties of a restaurant critic only too conscientiously, and naturally, died of the local cuisine. Well, it's cold comfort for an aging young man who'd left his hometown of Nizhny Novgorod twenty years ago in search of fame and money. An excellent English-language obituary writer in Prague. An author of sober but profound words about the deceased. Not great—after a Soviet specialist school, college, PhD, fellowship in the States, Moscow journalistic fever of the nineties, elections, "vote or else!" . . . It was when that "or else" came that I got out. No, I didn't smell an opportunity. I smelled a rat, or more precisely, a mouse; little mousy bureaucrats together with former KGB majors came and started to teach me (and everybody else) that we'd get there step-by-step and as for failures, the werewolves were to blame, and so I gave up. I dumped it all and got stuck between T. G. Masaryk and the Staropramen beer. I'd run away from the Russian Big Brothers, but didn't get anywhere. I fell asleep on the run and dropped down exhausted in a small apartment in the Jaromírka district of Prague. Every seven minutes, a tram rattles under the windows that look out onto the street. The back of the house, which looks like a servants' entrance, gets a blast of the noisy rumble of an electric train every ten minutes. A life between the rails. And above the roof there's the fat Nusle Bridge, the belly of which hides another railway with carriages — the underground. Rumor has it that this bridge used to be a popular place to commit suicide. There was a time when they were dropping down from it in clusters. I can imagine it — you go out to the balcony to have a cigarette, and there in the wreath of brains lies the brain of your rejected lover. What do I know, it might well be that it was the spirit of this place that had inspired me to become a full-time obituary writer for the local expat newspaper. By the way, the flying folks don't use Jaromírka these days; a special net was put up on the bridge, so the desperate now have to seek out other bridges as well as roofs and towers, in addition to other means of self-destruction — ropes, handguns, and poisons. Or gas. Mr. Lengthy here, did he kill himself or was it an accident? I ran through the staff notes about their headmaster again: found in the garage, in his car. A tragic accident. Death by suffocation. Why was he in his car? Why did he turn on the gas? Was he drunk? He was British, after all . . . I opened the attached photo. Well yeah, could be. Rosy-cheeked, a true pub regular from Harry Potter's Kingdom. As a headmaster he most likely didn't frequent bars here. Probably drank at home. A bachelor. Got drunk and imagined he was James Bond. Went to the garage. Crawled into the car. Kept pushing various buttons while picturing his Audi shooting out rockets, dropping mines, and growing wings. Tired out, he fell asleep and woke up in the other world.

"Good evening, Mr. Lengthy!"

"Good evening! What is this place?"

"It's Paradise, sir, a special paradise for British citizens. As you see, you can have the good old draught ale, here are the newspapers, a TV with the Premier League on, and you can refresh yourself with fish and chips over there in the corner."

"Thank you, sir. Do you happen to have anything stronger here?"

"In general, my dear Mr. Lengthy, we don't encourage such things, but taking into account your fruitful activities in the field of the dissemination of ideals and customs of the English society, we can allow for a little rule breaking. If I remember correctly, sir, you prefer brandy?"

Christ, what nonsense. I must've fallen asleep with my laptop on my knees. Enough. We can put it off for a while. I still have three days left to hand it in.

The next day I rang the Private British School to nail down some of the details of the late Mr. Lengthy's life. Of course, of course, Mr. Taborsky. Such a loss for us. Yes, yes, we've sent you everything you'll need for the obituary. Nothing to add. A detail? A striking detail? Hmmm. You might be interested—the Russian students of our school called him "London dandy." Yes, yes, in Russian— "*dan-dee long-dong-ski.*" You understand Russian? Oh! Excellent. Mr. Lengthy wasn't a fop, no, don't imagine that please, but he did dress in an impeccable way, and he took special care of his hands. A little old-fashioned, isn't it? But he had his own opinion of this. He used to go about with a nail file and in a free moment, of which as a headmaster he did not have many, believe me, he filed his nails. Our students had various views of this, but one girl from Russia remembered your greatest poet, a line of his in which he writes that it's no shame for a man of business to care for the condition of his nails. You, naturally, know this poet? *Push-keen* by name. Have a good day! If you happen to need any other information, don't hesitate to call and ask for the deputy head, Ms. Dudley-Oldborne.

The beauty of the headmaster's nails helped me a lot in creating the obit: I inserted it in place of the Falklands veteran's scar. So I got the extraordinary life of Her Majesty's subject, teacher and man of business, full of professional achievements. Born in Cardiff. College in Glasgow. Service in the Marines. Teacher of language and literature. Founder of the first international school in Prague. Took active part in the life of the British expats' community. Had an excellent knowledge of Czech language and culture. Single. Next of kin — none. Last rites to be held in the local Anglican church, then the coffin with the body will be sent to Cardiff and buried next to family members. And who will the school go to? There was nobody I could ask and no reason to do so.

Unlike the late Lengthy, I have a shit knowledge of the Czech language, which doesn't improve the attitude of the native population towards me, especially of the native authorities. But I've got to deal with them. Unfortunately. Sometimes I have to write an obit of some Czech hotshot related to the *Prague Herald*. This means having to crawl through the indigenous internet or ask a lot of questions. That's the job. I don't have the money to get a teacher of Czech but I force myself to watch TV and listen to the radio. So as not to expose myself to temptation, I've even denied myself satellite TV with its thirty English-language channels. When I sent Lengthy's obit to editorial, I made a cup of tea and sat down to watch the evening newscast on Nova TV. Train crash on the Pilsen line. Attack on some Gypsy in Moravia. Fight near a nightclub in Prague. Disappearance of a patient of the Bohnice lunatic asylum. Should you happen to see this man, please ring the number . . . A second before I switched off the TV, I focused on the photo. When the screen lit up again — damn old box, slow as hell! — a slovenly brunette was giving the weather forecast. Twenty degrees Celsius, rain. No problem here, but the missing mental patient was a spitting image of my Lengthy.

What distinguishes a professional obit writer is persistency and ability to find information. Jamie told me about this in his time, having commemorated tens of thousands of chosen deceased on the pages of all possible British newspapers. I met him here in Prague, he'd come to "get a breath of fresh air," to "have a pint or two," and in the meanwhile to gather material for a new edition of his *Lusty Traveler*. With a beer in hand we started talking and when it came out that we both wrote travelogues, the meeting turned into a serious drinking bout. I walked Jamie to his hotel in the Wenceslas Square. At the entrance, waving away the prostitutes swarming around us, he spent hours persuading me to take up "this business."

"An obit, mate, is an immortal genre. It's very simple. Listen. First, people are dying all the time. We won't see the end of it, at least not in the near future. Second, the absolute majority of the deceased had a family. Third, again, the absolute majority had a job. Consequently, there'll always be somebody who wants to say a nice word or two about them. Well? The thing is that the mourners cannot say, that is, write this word. It's a disaster! The limp-tongued morons strive to put one word next to another in memory of their never-to-be-forgotten Tony or never-to-be-forgotten Mary, but to no avail! And this is the moment when you walk onto the stage: tactful, educated, with a literary skill, capable of sharing the grief and paying the tribute due. They tell you what they need you to write and within an hour you create a masterpiece that deeply moves everybody around. They shower you with money and you disappear, whistling—right up to the next deceased person. Andrew, this position is simply created for you, you'll be the first in this city!" The traveling obit writer's arm embraced the nighttime square, including Saint Wenceslas' horse, imbecilic tourists, drug addicts, whores, and drug dealers, full of the all-pervading smell of fried sausages and sprinkled with empty beer cans, McDonald's paper bags, and cigarette butts. Jamie's raptured drunken gaze stopped at a short Gypsy woman, who was surveying the passing men. "*Ej, bejby, pojd' sem, kolik bude stát jeden polibek Rómky?*"[1] I didn't try to stop him. After all, the author of the *Lusty Traveler* has to carry out some indispensable field research, if the new edition of his useful and socially important book is to contain true and precise facts. The next day I set out for the newsroom of the *Prague Herald* to offer my obituary-writing services to the Prague English-language community. Jamie told me back then that the profession of an obit writer demands—besides a modest literary skill—the habits of a detective or a medievalist.

"You've got to know how to work with a document. With a source. To extract everything you need. And to select necessary in-

---

[1] "Eh, baby, come here, how much for a Roma girl's kiss?"

formation for the obit. That's all."

I'd read hundreds of detective novels in my time, dedicated myself to medieval studies at the university, and had recently heard
about an annoying academic article which combined the pompous
word *evidence* with the sprawling *paradigm*. That was probably why
I immediately became fond of my new job, much more than I was
of the politically zealous drivel with which I'd tortured myself and
my readers during the previous decade in Russia.

All this meant that when I missed the photo of the Bohnice runaway, I found it on the internet within five minutes, on the site of
Nova TV. I opened both pictures on my screen: the missing loony
and Mr. Lengthy. Never had I seen two faces so much alike. There
were tiny differences in details, but I'd known about those before.
The happy Lengthy had his legendary scar peeking out of the col-
lar of his pink shirt. Even the blurred photo made it clear that he
took meticulous care of his hands, and the shape of his nails was
impeccable. The lost patient didn't have a scar; as for his hands, the
photo didn't show them but it was more than obvious that the Bohnice orderlies hardly did his manicure. I was musing on this strange
similarity of the two people and mechanically leafed through the
archive of criminal reports on the Nova site. Oh, here's the incident with the British School headmaster. Let's see. He didn't answer
phone calls. They had the police involved the following day. Smell
of gas near the garage. They broke down the door. Want to watch
the video? Why not. Not a bad house for a humble teacher . . . The
scowling policemen, I can well imagine what they were saying to
each other about all those foreigners who've come here to our country and are growing happily fat, and we hardly make enough for a
plate of dumplings, and the beer's getting more expensive every day!
And now go drag their dead bodies . . . Stop. The camera operator
had manners and didn't shoot the face of the dead man, who was being pulled out of the car, but his hands were recorded. Filthy hands
with a trace of dirt under the nails.

The obit writer turned into a detective and set out for the mortuary the next day. Thank God, they give out press passes even to

those who write, not only about the living, but about the lives and labors of the deceased. So I had a formal excuse for a conversation with a cheerful little man with hairy legs in sandals poking out from underneath a crumpled doctor's coat. Jamie would sometimes supply me with credentials of various British newspapers as soon as I (prompted by him, of course) began to create for them the bios of exceptional deceased Czech figures naturalized in the United Kingdom. I told the man I was working for the *Sunday Post* and some distant relatives of Mr. Lengthy. I had to see the death certificate. Was there a postmortem? Alcohol in the blood? Nothing suspicious? Yes, a sad death for the hero of the Falklands War. What war? My monstrous Czech was apparently at its worst that day. The Falklands. Malvinas. You remember? Margaret Thatcher. The Argentinian junta. Mr. Lengthy was wounded there. Surely you saw the scar on his neck? No? No scar? That can't be. Not resembled a gentleman at all? No, you're wrong—Mr. Lengthy was a real gentleman and he took great care of his appearance. I said that, cunningly looking at the prosector's mane that badly needed washing. He obviously felt the sting and decided to strike back. That gentleman of yours had the hands of a digger.

Doctors of philology aren't the only ones for whom the knowledge of literary tradition is a necessity. An "obituary" is a literary genre; it has its own rules and its own poetics. A dabbler won't write you a good obit. Moreover, some of the best authors felt quite at home in the strict framework of this genre. And as far as detectives go, Holmes, who never picked up a novel, was wrong. A detective must know his letters, it stimulates his imagination and a detective without imagination is professionally useless. On my way home from the mortuary, I remembered that once before they'd buried a hobo instead of a gentleman. In a Dorothy Sayers book. And I remembered again how here, in Prague, a certain mister wanted a homeless guy he'd murdered buried in his place, only the mister and the police didn't quite agree as to his identity. It was this disagreement that killed the desperate Nabokovian hero. Fully in accordance with the laws of literature, I made up a dull excuse and visited Ms. Dudley-Oldborne.

Wandering for half an hour among the unbearably boring nine-floor apartment houses of the Bohnice district, where Lengthy's filthy-handed lookalike had escaped from the lunatic asylum, I came across a flow of English-speaking and English-giggling teen-agers. Going determinedly against the current, I found myself next to a great school complex. Big, expensive cars were parked by the gate; the younger students, having said goodbye to their friends in the universal language, ran up to the cars and exchanged bits of conversation in their mother tongues with the parents standing next to them. I waited a little in this youthful international atmosphere, which, if I was to believe the advertising leaflets, cost fifteen hun-dred euros per month. Well, the wealthy can afford to be cosmopol-itan. By the way, unlike their children, the parents didn't aspire to cosmopolitism, especially my fellow countrymen. Their fat watery faces were shining with contentment and self-assuredness—feel-ings universal enough, but here also having a specific native under-tone to them, impossible to mistake for anything else. They looked like they'd just shared a substantial sum with an accomplice and then drank and ate nicely with him—while the accomplice, the drink, and the canapé were all without a doubt of Russian origin. A portable post-Soviet Russia on the background of a British school in Prague. But never mind, because I was already on the flight of steps where the lady of the manor stood, a rosy-cheeked woman of about forty in thick ivory glasses. Could I see Ms. Deadborn-Oldly? If you're looking for Victoria Dudley-Oldborne, that's me. Oh, a thousand apologies. I'm the journalist who wrote Mr. Lengthy's obituary. Once more, I apologize deeply ... Not at all, not at all! How can I help you? I've brought the issue of the paper with the obituary, it may come in handy for the school archive or museum. So kind of you, thank you. Would you like a cup of tea? I won't refuse. Let's go to my office.

We marched past a long corridor, with posters hanging all over that encouraged political correctness and help for the suffering chil-dren from the third world, and then found ourselves in a smallish office. She offered me a cup of disgusting cheap tea and tasty Scottish biscuits (oh, I do know about these things!), and looked at me questioningly. I remained silent for some time, then cleared my throat, nodded to the black-framed portrait of Mr. Lengthy, and asked how the funeral had gone. Ms. Dudley-Oldborne had no idea, the matter was dealt with by distant relatives of our dear headmaster living in Wales. Believe me, it was more than enough for me when I had to go to the mortuary to identify the body. She sighed. Taking into account all the circumstances of the tragedy, you understand yourself how hard it was. The deputy headmistress sighed again, examining me all the time with her gray eyes, monstrously enlarged by the fat glasses of her spectacles. Phew. Then I organized the goodbye ceremony here in the chapel; thank God, the body was already in a closed coffin, because seeing it was something horrible . . . So sad, so sad. You know, they found him only on the following day . . . I'll tell you honestly, as soon as I saw that black and crimson scar on his neck, I immediately fainted. Awful. You see, I'd been at medical school, and was accustomed to mortuaries, but this . . . He was well loved here, we were all proud of the school, it's the best British school in Central Europe, things are going great, and suddenly, such a death . . . Why *such* a death? Unexpected, so unexpected. You know, all these doubts, did he actually do away with himself? . . . Yes, but there was alcohol in his blood . . . You're right, and to be honest with you, he was quite a heavy drinker, but that, strange as it may seem, speaks against all those horrible rumors. Well, thank you for the newspaper, I'll walk you to the gate, it's quite easy to get lost here.

The flight of steps was now empty. The cars had departed. My eyes swept through the little yard, the school building, and the football pitch, and I turned to her. What a pity this semester will see the end of it all! No, no, don't imagine anything! Nothing's happening to the school! And who's running it all now? Mr. Lengthy had written his last will long before—he left the school to his assistant, she's an experienced person, energetic and capable. Everything's all right with the school; things will go well, as usual. The sun had already set behind a massive cloud in the west, the evening had come, and a single playful scarlet sunray tore through the dark-gray rampart, setting ablaze the school windows and the large glasses of the deputy headmistress. Dudley-Oldborne's voice rang with assurance. I took my leave.

The contemplation of why she was lying took up the rest of my evening and a good part of the night. And lie she did—the poor guy who'd been buried in the Cardiff soil that very day had dirt under his fingernails and no scar on his neck. I could swear that it was that Bohnice patient. But what about the headmaster? Where did Mr. Lengthy hide? I finally fell asleep at dawn and dreamed about retelling the plot of *Lolita* to Sherlock Holmes, played by Jeremy Brett. Holmes was puffing away at his pipe, his eyes closed peacefully, and then he said: "Interesting, dear Taborsky. Very interesting . . . for the Americans. Here in England, Scotland, Wales, Ireland, and the Isle of Man, we've got many such villains. Could you please open my card file, the drawer labeled with *D*. Oh, yes, that one. Thank you. See here, for example, Charles Dodgson, a mathematician and photographer. No, no, he hasn't done anything bad yet. I'm keeping him handy, just in case." I was woken up by the phone ringing—they wanted me to come to the editorial room as soon as possible.

The dream turned out to be a prophetic one: the *Prague Herald* was having the first scandal in its ten-year history. A US-based organization called "Stop H. H.!" had sent the editor in chief (and cc'd the Prague police directorate) a respectful letter, announcing that visits to pedophilian websites had been made from an editorial computer of such and such number and payments for these visits were carried out through such and such debit card. And we ask you to look into this and take measures. The editor of the Society section had managed to escape from Prague unnoticed immediately after the phone call from the editor in chief—not only unnoticed, but rather quickly as well. We had to take out his things from the desk drawers in the editorial room and throw them into a big plastic bag that the police were to keep until all facts were established.

The position of the "stopped H. H." was offered to me—not only his working desk with the computer, printer, and the calendar of the Little Buddha restaurant on the wall, but his position on the staff of the paper. "At least temporarily," said the editor in chief and handed me the contract to read. The salary was rather substantial, so I signed and prepared to promptly react to the most burning problems of Czech society that were related to the English-speaking foreigners with a substantial income and a good appetite. The next day at work I set about cleaning the computer's memory of the little internet snags that had settled there which, it seems, had so painfully scraped the tender flesh of my predecessor. I'd almost cleaned up those pedophilian Augean stables when suddenly a bookmarked link caught my eye. It contained the phrase "London dandy." "Dandy," I thought, "dressed like a London dandy. *One may be a man of reason, and mind the beauty.*"[2] My mouse pawed the link.

Oh, was he a lusty man! My poor grasp of Czech didn't allow me to understand all the particular activities in which my dear Lengthy (now truly a part of my life!) wished to engage with the local underage girls for modest sums. Even the dictionary was blushing. I copied the site's address into my cell phone and killed the last of the vermin in the newspaper's computer. It was now clean. On the contrary, the footsteps of the headmaster's erotic adventures dirtied my own laptop. Our dandy was well-known, even popular, among the poor souls selling themselves on the internet market. I entered "London dandy" into a Czech search engine and came across the blog of one of them, where she described the difficulties of her meetings with this worldly uncle. The legendary nail file got a mention, too. Even the wondrous size of the headmaster's tool was discussed; too bad the girl in question and her colleagues didn't know the "prolonged" surname of their client. I was sick, physically sick, as if I'd filled myself on pork soaked in fat. There was Evil radiating from the screen—undiluted and pure, such as doesn't allow any justification. This Evil was intentional and cynical and its appearance before my eyes prompted me to only one thing—to do something as soon as possible so that *this* would be no more. I remembered the

---

[2] Alexander Pushkin: *Evgeny Onegin.* Translated by James E. Falen.

school, crowded with children from rich families, and I thought about the money of their parents being used to buy other children for that monster. Generally, I'm indifferent to instances of social injustice, but this was something else. My tranquility was destroyed by that horrible symmetry—money paid for educational activities converted into money paid for pedophilian ones. And once again I set out to meet Ms. Dudley-Oldborne.

Yes, it seems, he was certain nobody would catch him. You see, the Czech world and the expat world hardly overlap in Prague at all, especially the world of respectable foreigners and that of cheap prostitutes. The representative of the former may descend into the circles of the latter but the inhabitants of the netherworld will never be heard of in the upperworld. We all adopted this law long ago in Britain. And so did Mr. Lengthy. The deputy headmistress stirred her tea, put away the little spoon, and took a sip. It was by pure accident that Lengthy was caught by our security guard. His daughter would make some extra money by prostitution every now and then—the father didn't know about it. The guard says she wanted to leave the country and go to Britain or Ireland or America, wherever; she just wanted to get out of here. Lengthy didn't know whose daughter she was and gave her an English textbook with the stamp of our school in it: if you want to go to England, you'd better study the language. The father noticed the textbook. He thought she'd stolen it from somewhere in the school, although he'd forbidden her to come here. But she never did. He's a hot-tempered man, he probably beat her and she confessed everything. He recognized the client from her description, and came directly to Mr. Lengthy.

She looked at the black-framed portrait and let out a sigh. I was afraid I might jump up and start yelling, furious as I was, so I sat there in silence, systematically bending and unbending the teaspoon under the table. Yes, so he came to Mr. Lengthy and started blackmailing him. He didn't want too much—only that his daughter be accepted into the school free of charge. Poor Mr. Lengthy! He could never agree to that and so he decided to tell everything to me. He could never agree to *what*? Mr. Taborsky, you can see yourself, our students' parents wouldn't suffer a guard's daughter to study together with their children. My people, well, whatever, they turn up their noses but pass over it in silence; there's no other British school here and nothing would make them enroll their children at an American one. But your own fellow countrymen, Mr. Taborsky, are socially sensitive people, and unrestrained too. They wouldn't put up with such social mixing. No, it was definitely impossible. You know, poor Mr. Lengthy suffered a good deal. Said he understood the guard but couldn't do anything about the matter. The time was running out, the guard pressed further, Mr. Lengthy was very upset, he started imagining the police were after him, and that his office was being bugged. I was the only person he trusted and he even promised to sign over the school to me, if only I could find a way out of this unpleasant situation. Half of the school's income, naturally, would go to Mr. Lengthy. He said that everyday troubles were not to mar our important educational and cultural mission. Beautiful words, aren't they, Mr. Taborsky?

The teaspoon in my hands broke in two. I put both pieces carefully on the chair next to me and started tying a knot from a paper napkin. And so we were walking in the nearby park, you know, it's not far from the hospital, we were discussing the next steps and suddenly, you won't believe this, Mr. Taborsky, another Mr. Lengthy came out from the bushes. Of course, he was dressed differently, wearing some torn, dirty pajamas, his hair spiking out in all directions, but the face—the face was the same. And then it dawned on me. You know, Mr. Taborsky, I'm proud of that moment. The plan was born in my head in all its perfection, just like Athena was born from the head of Zeus. At that moment I was even smarter than Athena herself! Mr. Lengthy couldn't begin to understand why I struck up a conversation with the homeless man, especially when I started to feed him the whisky I always carry around in my flask, but then he got it. Mr. Taborsky, a clear mind and quick reactions— that's what made it possible for Mr. Lengthy to create such a wonderful school! I dropped the paper knot onto the floor. My mouth was dry but I didn't want to ask her for more tea. Well, and then we lured him into the car, drove him to Mr. Lengthy's house, and let him drink a lot more. The homeless man was a bit strange—he giggled all the time and sang songs. Then he fell asleep. Further, as you see, Mr. Taborsky, it was all quite simple, I'll skip the details. I'm only sorry that we didn't manage to clean him properly, otherwise you wouldn't have noticed anything ... Oh God, but why did you do all this? Mr. Taborsky, don't disappoint me now, you've figured it all out to the point of catching us and yet you don't understand anything. The headmaster's dead; most likely he couldn't bear the shame and committed suicide. That means there's nobody to blackmail anymore. The dead body in the car was a message to the guard. The case is closed. The school's saved. And what about him? Who, the guard? He carries on working, what else can he do, sitting in his glass booth at the entrance. We'll find a substitute for him next year. I know you're curious. I can even answer the question you dare not ask. No, no, I'm not afraid that you might go to the police. The Czech police aren't interested in runaway lunatics and rich Brits. Nobody will believe you, all the more so because you've got no proof. They won't go and open up the family vault in Wales! So I can tell you where Mr. Lengthy went. He's in Sri Lanka. A beautiful island, our former colony. Mr. Lengthy has multiple organizational and educational skills, it'd be a shame not to use them. He's going to head a fund to help the local children who've suffered in the recent tsunami. I think everything's going to work out beautifully for him. Mr. Taborsky, our former headmaster is an amazing person!

Leaving the school, I cast a furtive glance into the guard's cubicle. A scowling Czech of about fifty with a moustache was reading a tabloid magazine. The headline on the first page promised fresh insight into the private life of singer Karel Gott.

There was little work in the Society section. I lazily edited amateurish pieces about the long lines in the foreigners' police department, and pickpockets on Prague trams, read letters to the editor, and wrote obituaries in all the free time I had. Traces of deep scars on my left wrist were the only thing that reminded me of the shock I'd suffered, because I'd stuck my nails into it during the final phase of that conversation, so as not to strangle the bitch. All in all, I'm not part of the making of this evil. Or of evil in general. And really, where should I go? Who should I tell? Maybe a priest, but that's not my cup of tea ... I typed the password and opened my editorial mailbox. A message from our regular correspondent, Pete Glitter. His usual stuff on some socially important topic. Well, let's have a look. CZECH CAROLS AT THE EQUATORIAL CHRISTMAS. All right then. "Ms. Victoria Dudley-Oldborne, headmistress of the Private British School, has announced that a home for musically gifted orphaned girls is being opened in Prague. The funders include well-known international companies operating in the Czech Republic. At Christmas, a choir formed from the girls in the home will perform in Sri Lanka at charity concerts, arranged together with a local fund of assistance for children who have suffered from the tsunami."

Obituary

"That's the best possible place for my iconostasis. Brick wall, pipes, rails, and there, just imagine, my row of archangels: all the Bushes, Mugabes, Medvedevs . . ."

"To be honest, I see it all differently. You need a huge, magnificent hall, such as they have in the State Hermitage Museum: fanfares, gilt, hustle and bustle all around . . ."

"No, dear Andrei, no! Your artistic imagination is wholly conditioned by historicism. Of course, you studied history in college, just like . . . what's his name . . . you know him . . . Petya, yes, Petya, who used to hang around with the Jesuits here."

"Well, thanks a lot for the comparison. We know he's a real historian. I'm just a sickly man looking for his thirty thousand crowns a month . . . but still, just try to imagine: the Hermitage, decorations, a Rio carnival of the highest echelons of power!"

"Well yes, and real Komar with his Melamid. But never mind now, we're here."

We turned towards a wide gate opening onto the empty street that had just seen a herd of white-collars gallop by. There are no living quarters in this part of the Karlín district, so the nightly post-six o'clock emptiness acquires a dreamlike quality in being complete, like in a painting of Magritte's or of that Dutchman or Belgian—I can't remember—who painted a street, pretty much like a street here in Prague, it's all made in light-gray tones combined with yellow and light brown, it seems to be October and looks like rain had just passed, little puddles of water here and there, and above the houses there's a huge zeppelin, absolutely foreign, newly come, newly flown to the place from another world, a probe from a strange, cold, advanced, alien civilization, which has been sent here to check how things are going, whether we should be exterminated at once, ground into powder, rooted out, sprinkled with interplanetary dust, or whether we can be left a little longer to belch, flex our muscles, roll around in our own shit; however, in the street there's a group of four gentlemen in light-colored coats, some of them have taken off their hats and are waving them in the wind, greeting nobody knows what. What's obvious from the scene is the lack of understanding of both what is happening and of the destiny awaiting the gentlemen. And of the destiny awaiting us. I turned away from this visual image in my mind, shook it off from my eyes, and looked around. There we were, in the yard, in front of a huge factory built of red bricks that had grown dark with years, with an iron gate; on the left was a wasteland with the remains of artefacts of production; on the right stood another former factory but very tiny, like the famous asbestos factory that Kafka had been ordered to own. It was completely empty with just a small flight of stairs (added later), and a one-room apartment: curtains in the windows, laundry drying on the balcony, and flowers blooming under the laundry. But that's not where we went.

Efim Ilyich rang the bell and the door opened with a long squeak. A sly-looking guy with bluish-black hair wearing narrow, green pants gave us a big smile and mumbled *"Ahoj, Efime!"*[3] and let us in. So we entered that parthenon of the industrial period. Of course, I'd been to functioning factories before—a Ford car company, good as can be; I'd been to former factories too, disemboweled, polished, and lit by a different type of industry, consortiums of contemporary art, whose cynical generals show beyond any doubt that they dash out their goods in very much the same manner as Ford made his cars. But this was something different. This former assembly factory, or whatever it was—a huge space with cranes and ornamental ironwork on the windows, with stitches of railways that suddenly sprang up from the cement floor, led in their crooked ways towards the corners, but died on the way having lost the last of their strength, and, never reaching their destination, drowned in cement without a trace, and with the remains of tin plaques with health and safety instructions hanging from the dirty red walls—this wasn't yet a space sanitized with a mercilessly respectful contemporary design; it wasn't yet sprinkled with the distilled water of glittering indifference by the priests of political correctness. This factory was empty, dusty, and beautiful, like a decoration for the film *Stalker.*

"You see, Andrei, even the poor have privileges here!"

[3] Hello, Efim!

"What privileges—except, of course, that when we're finally broke, we'll be sitting munching on bread rolls for fifteen cents and drinking pints of beer for a dollar?"

"Anywhere in London or Berlin this place would've been mummified by that bastard Saatchi or maybe some lesser bastard. Whoever. And you and I wouldn't be let in until the day of the biennale opening. And I wouldn't have been invited to hang my stuff here; by the way, these curators didn't invite me properly either, only after and apart from the contemporary ones . . ."

"Well, you aren't exactly an epigone to Neo Rauch . . ."

"I'm certainly not. Too old for that. And I paint better. Why would I now change my *dolce stil* for some anti-art?"

"Well, nobody's asking you to go for anti-art . . ."

"Yes, yes, dear Mr. Duchamp. My friend Miró. My darling Salvador."

"So, you like it here? You'll hang your angels high?"

"We'll have a look, dear Andrei, we'll have a look, we'll enjoy together the annual observation of the holy name of Andy Warhol in Contemporary Art."

Efim Ilyich left to negotiate with the curators and I went to enjoy myself. This year, the curators went out of their way when putting together the exhibition. All the local warriors against the bourgeoisie and its acolytes were present in this former Temple of Added-Value Production. Over there, Anubis, dressed in an army uniform, cuts off Che Osiris' gilded fists. Here's a video with the Carollian crazy teatime, with the difference that its protagonists are seated at a table on the top floor of an oil derrick in the North Sea. They're drinking, of course, thick black liquid that's flowing out directly from a pumpjack. The stream's running dry and the Hatter's having difficulties pouring the last few drops into a gorgeous Wedgwood cup, while following a heated exchange that's turning into a fight; a few guests are pushed overboard, and what appears suddenly from the sky but a helicopter carrying a little Putin with a big Saudi; they self-importantly walk down the steps, and our heroes bow to the ground before them, spreading the carpet under their feet, licking it with their amazingly long tongues. In the end Alice performs a striptease by a pole glistening with fresh oil.

The space was full of other decorations, too. An old-fashioned flip board marking each new victim in Iraq. A few obligatory Chinese fake-art products—shining, pretty, and silly. An inflatable rubber mermaid with its head stuck up its own tail. Here and there, big rusty chunks of iron were lying around, either leftovers from the time when this place was used for the construction of huge machines, or brought in by the local exhibition installers in our day. A lot of photos; snippets of pop music at a few places; to sum it up, the most common trash, produced by everyday life and, respectively, the art based on it. A waste dump. Efim Ilyich was right: this place produced no artistic or aesthetic agitation in my mind, nor historical contemplations either, except if we count as historical a few trite historico-philosophical thoughts about the decline of the surrounding world and the Sunset Boulevard of Europe. My interest here was rather anthropologic: I was trying to imagine the consciousness and the pattern of thinking of people who have hoarded up mountains of useless rubbish in the place where in the past, by the flames of welding fires, the clang of the moving cranes, and the regular roar of heavy mechanisms, big-handed masters had assembled some complicated machines that were predestined in their own turn to produce some apparatuses, designated for the construction of some even more important things that had no relation whatsoever to human life. The active a-humanism crowned with a tired-out, slovenly, and intentionally boring a-humanism.

Having arrived at this level of my usual misanthropy, I found myself in the furthest end of the gigantic factory hall; space was specially fenced out here for the sake of the installation of a "famous American artist, one of the most renowned names of Art Brut— Father Bob (b. 1958)." I'd wanted to turn back and go search for Efim Ilyich but—either from a stupid conscientiousness or simply out of boredom—I turned into the plywood maze. Pink and red lights were weaving in and out projecting a single line on the wall: "December 2, 1988. Gremville, Iowa."

The space was furnished so as to resemble a fragment of a school building—a corridor, a few nice classrooms, a bit of the gym. Probably an American school. Hanging from the walls were timetables and announcements; the classrooms were full of desks, chairs, blackboards, and geography maps. Here and there, small zones of upheaval were to be seen: chairs thrown about, a door hanging on one hinge, a worm of notebooks and textbooks peeking out of a schoolbag. Next to it glistens a red pool, one of many around here. Brown spots on the walls. I almost stepped on a pair of glasses on the floor right in the middle of the classroom, and recoiled. I got scared. It was obvious I was standing in a building where many people had been killed—only, there were no bodies left. It all seemed to have happened suddenly—somebody had broken in and ended the lives of pupils and teachers. When I looked more closely, I even detected the traces of bullets in the walls; some had stuck in the desks and one of them had gone through the bust of Abraham Lincoln and lodged in the wall.

Having made my way to the gym, I realized that I'd been wrong; there was a body. One. It was suspended, rather low, hanged by its neck on a hook, hammered in the wall, like a coat on a hanger. It was a young man with long hair, wearing shorts and a sweatshirt with the inscription "Guns N' Roses," his arms hanging helplessly along his body, his face was crumpled, his tongue had come out of his mouth and his eyes out of their sockets. The doll was made in unbelievable detail and at first I couldn't believe that what I saw was an effigy of a dead man, and not the man himself. I pulled at his wrist in awe. It was hard and cold.

I felt somebody's hand on my shoulder and made a frightened jump.

"Oh my God, Andrei, please excuse me! I'm not an apparition, no no, I'm real . . ."

"You did scare me. Here—this hanged guy, there—puddles of blood, and here comes somebody's hand on my shoulder. Urgh. Who is it, do you happen to know?"

"Who? The one hanging here or the one who hanged him?"

"He was hanged by this Dad Bob but who was . . ."

"Andrei, when you go to a Biennale of Contemporary Art, make sure you read the descriptions. First, these are places at which texts tend to be more interesting than the creations of this . . . er . . . art. Second . . ."

"I know, I know, second, without reading them I won't understand anything anyway. But I really don't want to understand any of this. Although you are, as always, absolutely, *absolutely* right. Okay, I'm off to read about our Daddy Bobby and his corpse."

"Come to the office after, I want you to meet somebody."

On December 2, 1988, in the town of Gremville, Iowa, twenty-four-year-old Nick Woker, having armed himself with an automatic rifle and a handgun, broke into the local school and killed fourteen pupils, a guard, and a teacher. Two more pupils were gravely wounded and later died in hospital. Another one gravely wounded was a teacher, Robert Glass. He survived but ended up in a psychiatric ward. The most surprising thing was that Woker was never caught, in spite of his being identified, of the tiniest little details of his life surfacing afterwards, and of the thousands of fingerprints and other things. He threw away the guns and disappeared before the arrival of the police. The national search, the aid from Interpol, the enormous effort of dozens of FBI agents, it all came to nothing. Some believe that Woker ran away to Mexico and still happily lives there in some Aztec-god-forsaken town. Others are certain that the psychopathic murderer (who else would break into a school and start shooting everybody he meets, but a psychopath?) committed suicide by jumping into a river or something of the like. At any rate, it seems that Nick Woker had no motive—he hadn't studied at that school, he'd never even lived in Iowa, he was a quite decent college math student, his girlfriends didn't complain about him, nor did his friends; he was neither a Satanist nor a drug addict. Nothing to explain him; even the sweatshirt with the logo of the then-popular rock band he was wearing on the fatal day was one he'd borrowed from a friend two weeks before. Nothing.

Here the story of the murderer ends and now starts the history of one who hadn't been murdered that day. A bullet found its way into the head of Robert Glass, but the doctors managed to keep him from taking off to a better world. The consequences of the wound and the shock were such that Glass lost his mind for a long time. While in the hospital, the history teacher started painting pictures. He was depicting infinite empty rooms, only just deserted by people; all the things seemingly still preserved a bit of human warmth—it could be felt even though Glass was an amateur artist. He painted a lot. The wretched teacher wasn't, in fact, doing anything else—ate, drank, slept, walked around, and painted. The doctors considered painting an excellent means of therapy and kept bringing canvases into the hospital, colors, and other (as a local jokester put it) "Van-Goghian paraphernalia." Glass's works were hanging in the hospital, a few exhibitions were even organized in the college in the neighboring Greenell. That's where a visiting lecturer— a well-known New York curator—noticed them. He took Glass in hand and in just about a year the empty rooms of the hapless lunatic were to be seen at exhibitions in London, Berlin, and even Prague among works by other madmen—the curator aptly marked his pictures as "Art Brut," the art of the insane. The crazy world held in high esteem the crazy man's crazy art; Glass's works sold for higher and higher prices; he was getting rich and his mind was definitely returning to normal. The painted rooms were becoming more and more artistic, with more and more things inside them, until finally, Robert Glass published a series of paintings, showing storage rooms, heaped floor to roof with junk. Things were piling in tiny little corners, sometimes in mercilessly shining electric light, sometimes in dim gray, resembling Welsh mountains shrouded in fog. Having arrived at this point, Glass departed from painting and took up installations.

The lengthy explanatory reading was wearing me out. The last page was hanging so low on the wall I almost had to kneel to read the end of it. I learned that this here is his very first installation. It precisely copies the part of the school where the tragedy happened—a few classrooms, a corridor, and the gym. The only difference was that, whereas the scene of the murder was in reality full of bodies and the murderer had disappeared, in Glass's installation the victims are gone but the villain is hanging in the noose. So, justice—and in this case, it seemed, it was the Higher Justice—had been gratified. The history teacher, Father Bob, as he was called in the school, did what the police together with the FBI couldn't do: he punished the murderer. Not a verdict of history, so to speak, but a verdict of the historian . . . I'd had enough. I hurried to the entrance, and found Efim Ilyich in a friendly discussion with some people.

"Here you are! What do you say?"

"Awful."

"And here's the funder of the awful, Tom Grants. Tom, my friend Andrei. Andrei, this is Tom. I'll leave you to speak English and I'll happily return to the friendly Slavic language—I need to discuss something with our Czech colleagues . . ."

The cunning portraitist turned away from us and started to fill the air with drawn-out, regular, and almost mechanically pro-nounced Czech words, mixing them with prolonged "*prosíííím*,"[4] pronounced at the end of his expiration. I was left face-to-face with a short-haired man of about my age dressed in jeans, a sweatshirt, and sneakers, with cheerful attentive eyes and a strange habit of lick-ing his lips. On hearing about my main job at the *Prague Herald*, he livened up.

"So you're the only master of writing English obituaries in the city?"

"Not a great honor, Mr. Grants, since we're the only English-lan-guage newspaper in the city. Of course, it's fun to work as Charon in Prague, especially being Russian . . . But people die here so in-frequently there isn't much to do. So, to compensate myself I write about contemporary art exhibitions, kindly brought to them by Efim Ilyich . . ."

"And which is more difficult to write?"

"Obituaries, of course. An obituary's like a sonnet—it has the strictest rules. And the bereaved take very seriously the style, word choice, and the facts. And here: *Insecurity of the Modern Man. Critique*

---

[4] prosím = please

of Post-Colonialism. Escape from the Media Space. What else? Oh yes, this one's popular now: 'the artist invested several years of his life into this project, making his home in a dog shelter . . .'"

"Invested? No; it's me who invested, not some artist!"

We laughed. I suddenly felt embarrassed for such a lighthearted tone of voice in the presence of the person who did spend his hard-earned money for this huge heap of cultural and anti-cultural trash.

"I was very impressed by the school installation."

"Right, it's the highlight of the biennale . . . I'll give you an idea: write an article about the exhibition in the form of an obituary for the hanged murderer . . ."

"Nick Woker?"

"Yes, yes, I think that's what he's called. Yes, Nick Woker. Excuse me now . . ."

He opened a device that seemed to combine a range of functions from a smartphone to an espresso machine, and started to click unbelievably fast on its screen with a little metal stick; it was sparkling with tiny lights and I thought that this is what should be exhibited here, these high-tech extraterrestrial devices, instead of the antiquated Dadaistic trash . . .

It was getting cold outside, and the emptiness was the same. This deserted part of Karlín at eight in the evening of a summer work-day — that's Prague at its best. I asked Efim Ilyich who that guy was.

"Andrei, you're younger than me by twenty-something years and you don't know an inventor of some computer technologies? Tom Grants — he's written and talked about all the time!"

"Efim Ilyich, I write obits, not news. Swear to God, I don't know! Some techno nouveau riche?"

"Something like that. Sold his business that he'd started about ten years ago and is now enjoying life, putting money into contemporary art. By the way, he bought a couple of my portraits."

" . . . ?"

"He's Irish! It was the Joyce family portrait: James, Nora, their crazy daughter, and young Beckett with round teacher-like glasses. And another portrait — of Pope John Paul, of course. Pastoral staff, mitre, and eyes overflowing with kindness . . ."

Efim Ilyich giggled. Why, I can imagine his portraits, those mitres in them, those kind eyes. An elderly Soviet artist, master of iconic portraits of Lenin, Brezhnev, Suslov, and Gorbachev, what he brought into his new life was the refined precision of a high-positioned craftsman, the Flemish love of detail, and an amazing Arcimboldian perseverance in the final elaboration of even the strangest idea. And so, instead of the *Politburo of the Central Committee of the Communist Party of the Soviet Union*, what started to appear was the *Politburo of the Central Committee of the International Community 2008*; *Revision Committee of the Contemporary Art*; *Participants of the 38th Meeting of the US Democratic Party Are Listening to Hillary Clinton Reading a Paper*; *The Hague Tribunal. A Smoking Break*; *The Burning Harvest. Picking of Opium Poppy in the Kandahar Province*; *At a Rehearsal. Mick Jagger Shows His New Dance to a Ballet Group*, and similar masterpieces of new-old-fashioned painting which, provocative by its perfection, has so far evaded the cannibalistic art critics, doing their best to "put it in some context." But curators and gallery owners decided to play it safe and Efim Ilyich, having grown fat on his most recent sessions of the State Duma, left Moscow, because he was fed up with it, moved to quiet Prague unnoticed, and made himself almost a model Prague citizen of some ancient, handmade, pre-war, even Austro-Hungarian type. Although, of course, he was getting bored to death here, so from that moment eight years before, when we met and talked for ages at the local exhibition of Pivovarov, our discussion on any and all topics was never interrupted for longer than a week. Efim Ilyich taught me to enjoy visiting local museums, various biennales and triennales, introduced me to a bunch of local artists, and I even began to scribble something about "contemporary art" for my paper and other papers as well. All in all, I could well picture what a kind John Paul was hanging in Tom Grants' residence now.

"Yes, yes, he paid for everything—the factory, the promotion, and all. And they promised to give him any item after the biennale."

"Has he decided yet what he wants?"

"Guess!"

"Dear God, not that . . ."

"Exactly. All of it—the plywood walls, the shot-through Lincoln bust, and the maniac in the noose."

"And the author? He's a well-known artist and the work must cost a lot!"

"And that's the thing—he offered it himself. You'll see the day after tomorrow. And you'll see Glass in person too. He'll come to the opening. So, Saturday at five?"

The opening was delayed for an hour, so we met almost all the exhibited artists in front of the closed door. They also introduced me to Robert Glass. The big fifty-year-old man with a shock of black hair extended his huge hand to shake mine. My knuckles cracked but I didn't show any pain and the artist didn't notice. I wasn't courageous enough to praise his work, although naturally, it was the only reason why anybody would want to look at that abandoned factory in the evening. I mean, what *do* you say?

Oh, Mr. Hus, what merry flames were hopping over your mane in Konstanz when they were burning you at stake!

Your Highness, the show of your cut-off head simply knocked me sideways! What an expressive face you made!

Mr. President! I'd give half the kingdom for the wave of your hand when the bullet shattered your skull!

I muttered something silly, like "it's produced an unforgettable impression . . . ," smiled, and fell silent. What on earth should I ask him more about? Where can I see more of your works? What lunatic asylum? Among what other lunatics? In that moment a string quartet, which had been seated on folding chairs right there in the dust, started playing. "Janáček," Glass said fondly. "Thank God it isn't Smetana!" said I and we laughed together, the door opened wide, and the chosen audience flowed to the tables with dewy glasses of Müller-Thurgau and Frankovka wines and mineral water standing on them. It seemed that only two people in the whole company were drinking the water and, of course, they were the two Russians. Efim Ilyich winked at me and held his glass high: "This is the water that Goncharov came here for! And what's more, he wrote *Oblomov!*" What a wise guy. He knows about my pitiful literary attempts . . . Let's strike back . . . "I'll go to Marienbad and write a novel-length obituary! Its title will be *The Exquisite Corpse* . . ."

In the meantime, the audience was silently dissolving in the long corridors of the exhibition. Only a few people remained standing by the tables—me and Efim Ilyich, a group of local gallerists, and the big Glass, who, smiling for some reason or other, was sipping wine. The steady murmur reverberated between the walls of the factory, strange acoustics of which were bringing in distant conversations and making incomprehensible what one's neighbor was saying. Bits and pieces of responses, bursts of laughter, legs rustling on the cement, it all crept into my ears. Efim Ilyich was talking at some cruelly tattooed young man in a sweatshirt with the inscription "KILL THIS CURATOR." Feeling that a solitary dinner in front of a documentary on the Arte channel would be more pleasant than the socialization with the representatives of the local art industry, I put my glass on the table and prepared my goodbyes. In that moment people began to appear from the exhibition maze with a worried expression on their faces. Their eyes were looking for somebody, they were strangely talking to each other, and my ear, practiced in the sounds of the drawn-out Czech language, caught the word *vůůůně.*[5] "We didn't get around to look at the stand with draught perfumes," I joked clumsily and turned to Efim Ilyich. But for some reason he looked upset—as did the audience drawing close to the organizers. "Something's wrong there . . . Peter," he turned to the tattooed boy, "Peter, there's something wrong. Let's go and have a look."

The source of the disquiet was located in the area of the Glass installation. When we approached, visitors, quite scared by now, were emptying the area, almost running from the narrow passage. They were all muttering something about a "smell"; some, recognizing Peter as the curator of the biennale, started to chaotically explain. An atmosphere of anxiety hung over that dark corner of the huge rubbish-filled building. For some reason I recalled the rooms in Glass's pictures. Not surprising, perhaps because we were actually

[5] vůně = smell

standing next to his creation. At last, we decided to enter: Peter, myself, and Efim Ilyich. Slowly, peeking into each one of the model rooms of the slaughterhouse, looking around, smelling around. The unpleasant, sweetish smell was getting more and more intrusive with every step. Something familiar, but half-forgotten ... "Like a Russian funeral," muttered Efim Ilyich, and I shuddered. Of course. The coffin with the beloved body, the next of kin, hysterical women, frightened children cowering in the corners; the crowd falls apart before the approaching priest. Whispers, silent crying, at times torn by loud piercing laments. Sweet, horrible, unstoppable like radiation, the smell of the silent body, the smell of rotting and decay ... Here we are in the gym. The stink has become stronger, there's no escaping it, thank God I didn't have time for lunch. Nausea. But strangely, nothing has changed here. The two mats, the wall bars, the basketball net on one of the walls; on the other — the softened body. The red spots on the floor, on the mats, on the walls. Suddenly it seemed to me that it's not color but blood, stale blood, and that's what smells here, but no, it wasn't that. Efim Ilyich was silent, but suddenly he realized something awful and pointed his finger in the direction of the effigy. Peter and I followed it with our eyes. Nothing. "Closer! Closer!" shouted the old man. Peter hesitantly moved towards the wall — and a swarm of flies flew off of the face of the hanged man. "Dear God, it's a body!" On the wall, with the rope on its neck, was hanging a real corpse, a body that had already started to decompose. Holding my breath, I drew closer. The same face as the day before yesterday, only with some strange white spots, as if it had been crudely smeared with greasepaint, the uncomely hair moved to one side, fingers turned blue. Peter was already back at the entrance; through the loudspeaker, the visitors were being encouraged to leave the building; we heard a police-car siren a few minutes later, but we were still standing there in silence and looking at the dead man. What followed was almost unimaginable. Efim Ilyich took out a Kleenex and rubbed it on the dead body's face. Creamy white dirt came off on it. Efim used the same Kleenex to pull the body's hair. A high forehead showed, as if the hair moved backwards. I'd never seen anything more horrible in my life. "Andrei, do you recognize him?" How can I recognize this figure? Has he gone mad? "Andrei, do you recognize him?" I glued my eyes to the artist, having decided that he's gone nuts. "Andrei, stop staring at me, and pull yourself together! Look, quick, do you recognize him?" I moved my eyes to the dead body. Of course not, how can I recognize … And then through the dirty greasepaint, through the ugly wig, through the whole terrible masque, I recognized the funder of the exhibition, the famous arts patron, Tom Grants. At that moment two policemen ran out from the corridor. Behind them, waving his arms, rolling his eyes, and even yelling something, Peter ran in. "Kill this curator," I babbled. Leaving the factory, I momentarily noticed Glass. Just like an hour ago, he was standing there and gulping wine from his glass. Apparently, he wasn't getting what was happening.

The press went crazy and not only (and not all that much) the Czech press. DEATH OF PATRON. MORTAL BIENNALE. ONE MORE DEAD BODY ON SCHOOL BATTLEFIELD. These headlines were traveling from paper to paper, from magazine to magazine, and the gems in their online versions went beyond disgusting. The Russian internet showed itself in all its beauty. THE PATRON GOT SAD, AND HUNG HIS HEAD—rejoiced *Belledejour.ru*. LET HIM HANG ON THE WALL A MOMENT LONGER—recorded the *Rumoroff* business issue. IF A PATRON IS HANGING ON THE WALL IN THE FIRST ACT … people from the Culture section of *Newstream* showed how well read they were. CNN distinguished itself once again, putting the coverage of the Karlín events under the Entertainment section. Intellectuals joined in later. Unfortunately, Derrida and Baudrillard had died, so the hard work of interpreting the incident was taken on by humbler personages. Žižek and Habermas somehow managed not to get involved; however, well-known art philosopher Ivan Klein cheered up the public with his article in which he called the dead body of Tom Grants "the greatest creation of the art of the early twenty-first century"—after the terrorist act of September 11, of course. Tanya

Creosote bravely announced that "by far not a symbolic murder of the patron tells us that the contemporary society is abandoning the old scheme 'artist—curator—gallery-owner—funder' for the absolute dominance of the artist." Finally, Damien Hirst himself said in the *Guardian*: "The death of the patron of the name Grants beautifully testifies that the times when art was parasiting off grants, is gone. It's time to make money, dear colleagues!" There were rumors that somebody was preparing for the regular Venice Biennale an installation in the form of a gallows, with effigies of the most famous patrons hanging from it, from the Roman Maecenas to Peggy Guggenheim.

The success of the investigation was much more limited. It was established that Grants had been strangled on Thursday night—it must have been immediately after Efim Ilyich and I left. The specialists couldn't even determine whether the funder was killed first and then his corpse was hanged or whether he was still alive when hanged. There were no secondary injuries. No alcohol, drugs, or poison were found in his body. Nobody had entered Glass's installation since that fateful evening, and the factory had been closed, so the murderer had full forty-eight hours to hide. He didn't even think it necessary to hide the traces of his crime. It was exactly this intentionality that amazed the investigators and criminal reporters. It was obvious that the culprit not only intended to murder Grants, but he also wanted to express something through his crime—otherwise why else take all the pains to create the dreadful? All the highbrow interpretations of what had happened stemmed from this particular fact. For some reason everybody was certain that it was an artistic deed committed by an underground artist who could be called a "realist" in the sharpest sense of the word. If the phrase "death of art" were still in use, he would most likely have murdered all his colleagues and consequently committed suicide. If the post-structuralist "death of the author" were being discussed, our hero would have done away with some renowned writer. But what did he mean by this? That was the question torturing the best minds of university departments of culture, museums of contemporary art, and intellectual institutions. Theories gave birth to other theories, while the police investigators had no real traces in their hands. There was only one person who could have answered certain questions and that was Robert Glass, but unfortunately, he wound up a secondary victim of the Karlín events. The murder committed at his installation, dedicated to murder, shattered Glass's fragile consciousness and he relapsed into quiet madness again. He was taken away to Iowa and put into the same asylum in which his artistic career had started. But he didn't paint anymore. During the new seizure of madness, Glass was gradually becoming a normal man again—such as he'd been before the fateful December 2, 1988. He ate well, went for walks, watched baseball, and read a lot of history books, as if he wanted to catch up with the twenty years that he'd spent out of touch with his first profession of a historian. Within half a year, he was well enough for the doctors to start talking about a release. A mandatary of his bought a house for him in the northern part of California; he had money, received in the past for the sale of his Art Brut masterpieces, enough for a pleasant life in the undemanding care of specialists. Efim Ilyich, who'd just returned from the States, told me all about it. He'd been to Iowa too, in the town of Greenell, where Glass's artistic journey had started. My Prague friend had his *Dr. House* series portrait gallery exhibited there; the demand for pop stars and politicians had plummeted in the past year or two and Efim Ilyich had to start on glamorous pictures of TV heroes.

"Do you mean you saw that poor madman?"

"I did."

"But how?"

"He found out about me staying in Greenell—and that's very near Gremville—and told somebody to ask me to come and visit him."

"But you hardly knew each other at all!"

"True, not much. But still, we'd met about three times here in Prague."

"How is he?"

"Great! Put on some weight, got healthy color in his cheeks and a self-assured look in his eyes. You know, Andrei, they feed them better in that asylum than in many a Prague restaurant . . ."

"Not much to boast about."

"No, no, don't start that, they have it really good. And a lovely garden, too. I'd go and lie in that asylum for half a year. I'd read so many books . . . And that's what Glass is doing—reading."

"Doesn't he paint at all?"

"He's forgotten all about it. He says he's happy to have got rid of that obsession, as he learnedly calls it . . ."

I was standing in front of a life-size portrait of Stephen Fry. The wit and erudite was pictured in a fancy frock coat with an order ribbon across his chest. On a heraldic band above his head was shining the inscription "Stephen II D:G:Br:Omn:Rex." There weren't any other pictures in Efim Ilyich's studio.

"Did he order it himself? Aspiring to royalty?"

"No, no, of course not. Some American Wodehouse lovers' association. Good, eh?"

I felt that the old artist wanted to tell me something but couldn't pluck up the courage to do so. He was visibly upset, moving from one place to another the teapot, cups, and an old-fashioned bowl of old-fashioned Russian jam that he treated me to every time. I always wanted to ask him where he got gooseberry from in this country . . . Instead I said: "Why did he ask you to visit him?" Efim Ilyich came to Fry, threw a blanket over him, turned around, looked at me, scratched his nose, walked up to the window, and said in a flat voice:

"To explain why he'd killed Grants."

"Beg your pardon?"

"To explain why he'd killed Grants."

I glued my eyes to the wall that had a number of nails hammered in. Some of them had drooped and I thought that Efim Ilyich should be careful about choosing those on which he wanted to hang the finished masterpieces. The artist himself was staring at the sunset, undisturbed. I gulped down the rest of my tea.

"And why did he kill Grants?"

I hoped that Efim Ilyich was joking, although I never knew him to possess any inclination for word games but still ... no, he wasn't playing a game. He was afraid of what he was saying, although he wouldn't let it show.

"He killed Grants because Grants was Woker."

"He killed a man just because the bats in his head imagined that the funder of the biennale in Prague was the same madman who'd almost murdered him in Iowa?"

"No, dear Andrei, he didn't imagine it."

"Efim Ilyich, stop frightening me!"

"I'm not frightening you ... I'm scared myself. But it's true."

"What's true?"

"That Woker was Grants."

"Can you prove it?"

"I can't. But Glass told me everything."

"What did he tell you?"

"That when he was recovering from his wounds, he decided to commit suicide. He'd been very fond of his pupils, particularly those that Woker had murdered. But then he realized that it was silly to kill himself after almost getting killed and, what's more, healed of his injuries. 'They would've cared for me in vain,' he was thinking, watching the doctors and nurses. Sensitive person, isn't he, Andrei?"

"They don't come more sensitive than that ..."

"Wait, wait, there's more!"

Efim Ilyich livened up, turned away from the window, walked through the studio, and sank into an armchair. I saw that he'd finally decided and damn all his fears. I sat down too, backwards on a chair, and got ready to listen.

"So, this is how he planned it. He pretended he'd gone crazy. Decided to wait in hiding for a few years, while they were searching for Woker—just like in Dumas' novels, he decided to take revenge. That is, to kill him. Knock him off, as you say. But he didn't know yet when he'd be caught. So he decided to lie low—it was you who taught me this wonderful expression!—in an asylum. The therapy was very light and humane; they weren't giving him any books to read. So he started painting whatever he saw. And he saw, mostly, rooms—they didn't let him out to walk for long yet and when they did, he was always being watched. Further it all happened by itself. Some phony curator saw his daub and decided to make money off it. He created a huge heap of bullshit—about "savior's complex," "Hammershoi syndrome," "post-intellectual storage of old ideas in an absolute de-humanized emptiness," and the like. And put our perfectly normal Glass down on the list of mad artists. And Glass didn't object to it! He was painting various spaces, people came to like him, he changed normal rooms for storage rooms, everything was selling well . . . Just one thing was amiss . . ."

"They didn't find Woker."

"Exactly, they didn't find Woker. And I don't know how all this would have ended, if it hadn't been for a coincidence. I think he'd have gone really crazy if . . ."

"Just don't say that Glass came across Woker in a line for coffee in the Starbucks."

"Why Starbucks? Try something bigger. Woker came to his exhibition in Berlin."

"This is getting very Dostoyevskian. Your favorite teacher's read too many books."

"That never hurt anybody, Andrei. Glass is certain that Woker visited that exhibition on purpose."

" . . . ?"

"Meaning, of course, that he didn't come as Woker the murderer, but as a mobile technology pioneer with an inclination for arts patronage, citizen of Ireland, Tom Grants. He came and bought a few of Glass's works."

"And he recognized Woker?"

"Immediately. He did, although he'd only seen him in the school for a few seconds. 'You can't forget that smirk,' Glass told me, 'and that ugly tongue, licking his lips.' You know, Andrei, he's sure that Woker understood, no, not only understood, but knew, and hoped that Glass would recognize him."

"This is not even Dostoyevsky any longer but some thriller with Jesuit psychology. What for?"

"Give me an easier question. I asked Glass and he responded very simply: 'Because he's mental!' Andrei, isn't this explanation enough? It's true, after all. The man killed eighteen people, just for the sake of it—isn't he mental?"

"Mental."

"But I have the answer for you. Glass thinks that Woker simply enjoyed the torture that he could, by this stroke of good luck, bring to the unshot teacher again."

"And then?"

"I've told you—he bought a couple of Glass's works. And then funded the exhibition at which Glass re-created the place of his crime."

"And ... Damn, he actually suggested that I write an article about the biennale in the form of an obituary for that hanged murderer ..."

"Aha! I didn't know that! Nor did Glass. Are you still in doubt?"

"Rather that ..."

"Glass caught him on his installation like a spider catches a fly. He knew that Woker wouldn't refuse a private, escorted trip to the crime scene. But Woker didn't account for the effigy in the noose. He saw it as a sign of desperation, but it was bait. A worm on a hook."

"And he strangled him?"

"Exactly, strangled. You and I went home and the funder went with the artist to have a look at the outstanding work of contemporary art. The artist came back alone. The funder remained hanging. He became art himself, so to speak. But that's all your business—art, patrons, messages, mediums ... I only know one thing. Glass told me: 'I hanged the murderer at the place of his crime. I'm happy.'"

"And cleverly hid the traces of what he'd done, that is—hid himself in the lunatic asylum."

"Of course! At the end of our conversation Glass joked: 'Now that I've done what I wanted to, I can start to live. A prison, especially a Czech prison, wouldn't serve me. You get me?'"

"And do you get him?"

"Of course. And he has my full approval."

I wanted to ask Efim Ilyich whether Glass wasn't afraid that somebody would discover him, catch him out, but decided to stay silent. Nobody will catch him out, a poor lunatic. But I had another question and I asked it.

"And what if it's all different? What if Grants isn't Woker and Glass is a paranoid murderer? Or else—what if Glass is a true madman and Grants was killed by somebody else?"

"That's a big maybe, Andrei. We'll believe that it all happened exactly this way. Dammit, one needs something to believe in."

CCTV

The economic crisis was raging, and I was standing on the second floor of the Renaissance shopping mall in the line for Thai fast food. There were two people ahead of me—a young man with an educated look about him wearing ivory glasses, apparently imagining he was in New York or Berlin, and a local clerk, a mix between a rabbit and a donut. The server gave me an old-acquaintance smile—why not, after all, I talk to her in English; the broken Latin of our times has brought us so close that we even wave to each other when we meet outside the mall. I mean, of course I don't recognize her at first—without her orange apron and the greenish light shining from the plastic boards with pictures and prices of the meals—but she waves first, so that I can't but wave in response. I am most respectful, it's my main characteristic. In order to be indifferent, you have to be respectful. In order not to lose your sanity, you have to be indifferent. And I don't plan on losing my sanity quite yet. So I mechanically wave back to her in the street, and only then do I realize who it is. Exactly! That server from the Thai bistro in the Renaissance. She always speaks in English, which is strange—so many years in Prague and she hasn't learned Czech, not even some "*objed-návka*"[6] or "*bohužel.*"[7] The Vietnamese, for instance, are perfectly fluent in a bird-like variant of Czech they invented themselves, the Chinese chirrup in their own way, and even some Americans. But not her. The Thai have their pride.

The intellectual took the box with the noodles home with him, the clerk got something hot with rice but I—in no rush and with a lot of thoroughness—treated myself to a whole lunch consisting of two meals: spring rolls, noodles, and even a bottle of alcohol-free beer. Yes, Clausthaler, please. As usual. She repeated the order to a huge young man with almost a mohawk on his head, the Thai punk grasped a decent-sized pan and started frying onion, soya shoots, and something else as well. The pan was emitting an overpowering smell but I don't mind, I'm fine, this is what I come here for. Yes, once a week, or twice, I go to the Renaissance—to eat Thai food, to walk

[6] "order"

[7] "unfortunately"

around the shopping galleries, to stare at the Czechs and Moravians, well dressed, well perfumed, one-dimensional under this neon sun, in the midst of plastic walls, aluminum constructions, mannequins, and gigantic advertisements for various underpants and lotions. Of course, not just the Czechs and Moravians—this place is frequented by Russian female tourists, and Ukrainian workmen washed of plaster and other dirt to celebrate the day off, and expat mamas with little kids. All with their own purpose in mind, but they all have— and so do I—also a common goal: to hide from the gray, decrepit city full of dog shit in this lively temple of consumer society, lit up and surgically clean. In this cheap paradise. After all, do we, people, need a lot? I certainly don't. Before, quite a lot of years ago, when I'd just moved here, walking around the Old Town, going to see the river by the Rudolfinum building, wandering around the crooked little streets lit by the dim windows of grubby taverns was what they call "the must." Of course, Prague, the capital of Central Europe, almost the capital of Europe as such. What good fortune to live here, under the canopy of hideous baroque, among houses where the idiot Švejk used to live, to pour down beer, polish one's bowels with slivovitz, get a kick from imagining that here's the new Paris of the twenties and you're, for example, a new Papa Hem or a new Henry Miller . . . A few years had been spent on dealing with this nonsense, no advance, no alehouse. Sobriety. Sobriety, a bottle of alcohol-free beer in the Thai fast-food joint, the shopping mall, similar to any other consumer circus in any European backwater. To sit at the plastic table of light-green color, poke with the plastic fork into the steaming hill of smelly noodles on the plastic plate, to wash down all this stuff with a flat, watery drink, my nose itching from the hops that the generous Germans stuffed into this fake beer to make it taste more like a beer and less like a fake. To stare—insolently at times, surreptitiously at others—at the public. Here, at the neighboring table, a girl with her boyfriend: they've dragged a whole bucket of fries from the Kentucky Fucken Chicken across, together with a smaller bucket of chicken limbs soaked in genetically modified fat, and a liter of Coke; they're sitting, cooing to each other, licking their fingers, feeding each other carcinogens. Sweet, loving, kissing. She, as they come, wearing a pair of jeans showing half her ass, rolls of fat overhanging the blue waist, bluish-black hair—she apparently puts more effort into dyeing than washing it. The boy fits in well with her—solidly built, his hair cut short, his pants showing his butt too, pale, covered in a few little boils. A little further away there's a family, the kids are squealing, running around the chairs on which the silent adults focusedly dip pieces of potatoes from the same KFC into mayo. From somewhere in the ceiling the favorite music of shopping malls is carrying to us—a little of Sting, a piece of bald Phil C., the duo of good old Annie Lennox, "In the Deathcar" by wretched Iggy. Again, one must give thanks to the heavens for not hearing some rapper the like of Half Dollar. Seriously, it's a paradise.

* * *

I'm a master of balance, I am. A backpack on my shoulder, in one hand, the tray with two plates that are trying hard to slip to the light-gray floor, plastic confusion of stunted knives and forks, and German ballast in the form of the Clausthaler bottle, crowned with a paper glass from Coke; if it weren't for the heavy-weight German piece, the plates would swim away for sure. Finally, the free right hand is opening the swinging lid of the waste bin that's shared across the whole hall of gluttony, goodbye lunch, all that's left is to wash my hands in the bathroom around the corner from McDonald's. That's it. Clean. Whistling *She loves you yeah yeah yeah*, through the food court, towards the escalator, step on the belt, trying not to forget myself and lean against the rubber handrail. And here's the clothes. There's everything here that the soul, that sweet wanderer, may wish for. Clothes in the "going out downtown" style, common and expensive. White and yellow polos with the brand crocodiles of Lafontaine crawling about. Miles and miles of crumpled mess, sewn together by Far Eastern slaves of either Scandinavian Adventists or Cypriot Scientologists. Suits from Yves Chateau. A faultless pair of pants from the Reverie company. Glinting black shoes by the excellent Laurent. Pa Ganuell No 5. Wayway from China and Heike from Japan. Rolling my eyes at the gleaming windows full of pale-bodied mannequins, I head for the Bentham and Engels, more suitable for my age and wallet, to seize the clothes of the departing summer that have lost any value by now. Looking at the advertising photo of a disheveled girl who, wearing a silly glittering dress, was sucking champagne straight from a bottle with a straw (*I die after every party*), I bumped into an old man with a walking stick. Pardon. Sorry. His rosy cheeks twitched in a smile and his wife dragged him further along the sparkling gallery—to buy, to buy, to buy. I wondered, do they know that any of the things they buy today could become their shrouds? That the death will prevail in any outfit—in gorgeous linen pants from Previous or a bathrobe by Duke Clarence, it won't spare the simplest shirt made by Czech seamstresses. It loves any and all, white, black, clean, drunken. As if sensing something off, the elderly couple turned around but I was already entering Bentham and Engels, excuse me, ladies and gentlemen, I never thought anything like that, goodbye to you.

I chose a few T-shirts and headed for the fitting-room area. Nodding to the scowling lady at the entrance, I got a few numbers from her and directed myself to a far cubicle. For some reason I take great pains not to show fragments of my body to people around. And that's in our wonderful Prague that in the summer overgrows with pale, hairy male flesh, peeking out from under too-short A-shirts and silly boxers that nowadays pass for shorts; bellies, thighs, calves—various tricks with the sole purpose of not covering this anthropologic shame, let the biomass breathe, open the world to it, open it to the world. Short-winded, ugly white people, pretending to be part of some Copacabana, what consequences would it have for all of us? for this world? where are we heading? Such were the questions I would've been asking myself had I any will to ask questions, but I had neither will nor mood to be asking as I hadn't had for a lot of years, so I limited myself to preventing pieces of my own body, superfluous for nearby eyes, from falling into the zones of perception, that is—non-perception of the people around. I drew the curtain and started to take off my T-shirt.

Reaching for the second-in-line discounted product of Messrs. Bentham and Engels, I dropped the first one, already discarded, and looked at the floor. Thick red liquid was making its way from under the dividing wall, moving slowly, carefully, taking pains to curve around the smallest bulges in the floor. As if somebody, zealously taking off their old outfit, broke a bottle of Heinz ketchup, bought in the same shopping mall (I immediately recognized that outstanding color!) and now the tomato muck is crawling into my private territory, teasing me, scaring me. Some Tarantino or whatever. But no, the red muck was progressing much faster than I'd imagine Heinz to move from a broken bottle, faster and somewhat more demandingly. I stepped back a little to the opposite wall, watching the red pool nearing my sneakers and finally, when I had nowhere to back away, I stepped over it, drew open the curtain and came out into the corridor. Not a soul there. The scowling lady who'd been playing at Cerberus only a few minutes before had dissolved in the spaces of B and E, and there were no shoppers to be seen in the fitting rooms, except the neighboring one. I cleared my throat, knocked on the dividing wall and tried to create a friendly tirade in the Czech language. *Promiňte, co za strašně červená*[8] . . . and so on in a wild Khlebnikovian dialect that in my mind stands not only for Czech but also a few other Slavic languages—all together in a pile, so to speak, in order not to get bewildered, should I find myself in Poland or in Serbia. But my linguistic pains weren't granted an answer. There was silence behind the closed curtain, not a crackle, not a sigh. I knocked again, dug up from my memory a few more formless bits and pieces of the Slavic—no reply. Only then did I take the risk of putting my head between the rather dirty curtain and the plastic wall and seeing what I saw.

She was lying like in a film noir: a light-haired girl wearing panties and black stockings, lying on her side, sticking her left ear to the floor, one arm thrown behind her head, the other extended upwards, as if she came first in some strange contest, broke through the finish line and there, in full stride, at the last breath, were taken by a bullet.

---

[8] Excuse me, what horribly red ...

But it wasn't a bullet, it sure wasn't. The blood was flowing from a long wound in her back, under her left shoulder blade, the little red stream found the shortest way through her body to the floor, formed a puddle, and from there the blood was moving further — under the dividing wall into my cubicle. It suddenly dawned on me that what I'd mistaken for Heinz ketchup must have reached the next fitting room, but there was nobody, so that I and I alone had to take measures. A red-and-blue striped dress was hanging neatly above the body, as if the soul of the dead woman were watching the abandoned body from above — that's the result of the wild surpluses of the Soviet self-education I thought, almost closed the curtain, stopped myself in time; for once the surplus of literature came handy: Sherlock Holmes dixit — don't ever touch anything at the scene of the crime. "But is it a crime?" a hopeful thought flashed in my head. Of course it's a crime. She was killed, you idiot; can't you see?

So I went to search for people. The most surprising thing was that there weren't any in the store. The territories of Jeremy B. and Friedrich E. had emptied perfectly, the space was full of endless rows of hundreds of tops, shirts, jackets, all crucified on coat hangers with unmistakable names on their necks — S, M, L, XL, XXL. The crowds of padded hangers gave way to rows of limply hanging pants: such was their march through the store — legs apart, chests apart, like characters from the 25th sequel of *The Zombies* movie. Those that hadn't been let to participate in the parade yet, were patiently waiting for their turn folded on the shelves. In the sound incense I identified the sweet Take That — " How Deep Is Your Love" pouring from the ceiling. In another situation it would've been fun to put all that together, to create a single picture out of it — shirts, pants, songs, e-v-e-r-y-thing, it was the reason why I was staying in this city at all, when the plot that had led me here was concluded, but it was all somewhat off, I mean, it's well worth it to come here especially for this but not now, dammit, where are you all hiding now? Behind the windows, along the galleries of the mall, people were walking, talking, smiling, making gestures, looking at me, at the hangers, at the mannequins, not showing any signs of surprise over the store being absolutely empty, with nobody there except some guy with his mouth open in astonishment. I even managed a nasty thought about how all the darlings will get scared when they find out what happened, what moiré noirs are going on here, what ketchups are being broken, what blondes are being murdered ... Fuck. Murdered. Is there at least somebody here?

I had a choice — either look for somebody in the recesses of Bentham and Engels or jump out, screaming at the top of my lungs, in the direction of the shoppers, calling for the police, ambulance, lawyer, prosecutor, priest. People's smiling faces on the other side of the store window made me decide for the former: how would I tell them? in what Khlebnikovian dialect? how many eons would pass before the morons would understand what had happened and what needs to be done? And then the police would arrive, gray, crumpled people with unwashed hair, wearing ugly uniforms. And I'd have to explain everything again. And the first person that they'll catch, retain, tie down and take to the police station will be of course myself and they'll let me out late, oh so late. So it's better to look for somebody here, tell them secretly about what happened in this fitting room of theirs, maybe even demand explanations, say, here I am, trying on your gear, doing no harm, and here's girls getting murdered, I almost soaked in blood in your store, this is something outrageous, I'll lodge a complaint, I'll turn to the court, requesting compensation of the moral damage, so. Having wandered for conscience's sake among the empty sleeves and empty pants, I headed for a door leading, as I believed, to the hidden administrative part of the store.

Behind the door started a long, light-gray corridor, along which were several more doors. Walking by, I tried the handles but to no avail, all were locked. The corridor ended with another door; when I approached, I saw it was ajar. I peeked into the crack — a man was sitting by the panel of Bentham and Engels video feeds wearing a gray-blue uniform and without moving was staring at the dozens of gray screens in front of him. On his desk was a simple meal with a bottle of Pepsi standing next to it, and a page of an unfinished tabloid magazine was hanging from the edge: the bright yellow and pink naked butt in the magazine and the blue and red label of the Pepsi somewhat brightened the generally mousy palette of the room. All right now, I'll have to disrupt this idyll, can't do anything about it, I opened the door, greeted him, and started to talk.

He was a dull man of about fifty years with a grayish face, irresolute mouth, and cold unmoving eyes. He turned to me in his swivel chair and silently listened to the wobbling story of the *mrtvola*,[9] about how the blood *dostala do mé kabiny*,[10] about how *v obchodním prostore nikoho nebylo*,[11] and so on and so forth in the universal form of Slavic that I use here, in the center of the Slavic world, in the center of Europe. When I stumbled, trying to remember the Czech equivalent of "wound," the man opened his soft mouth and respectfully suggested switching into English, should that make my task easier. Now it was me who was opening my mouth in surprise: it's a well-known fact that the Czechs not only don't wage wars—they don't speak foreign languages either, and any attempts by foreigners to speak a language other than Czech come to nothing through the murderous sentence: "You are in the Czech Republic, speak Czech." The guard of a local store (albeit originally British), suggesting switching over from his mother tongue into English—no, that cannot be. But that was and I, naturally, agreed.

Strangely, the information about the body lying in the pool of blood in a fitting room of their store didn't worry the guard much. He offered me a chair at the desk on the left side of the door, slowly turned in his own chair to the panel and focused on pushing the buttons. He asked me over his shoulder what time I'd entered Bentham, I answered, and within moments my own unhurried wander of twenty minutes ago came up on three of the screens. Here I am, opening the door of the store, here I'm turning to somebody, entering, deep in my own thoughts, here I'm walking lazily along the hangers with the garments, feeling this thing and that with contempt, here I'm picking two T-shirts and turning away from other customers, I head in the direction of the fitting rooms, here I give

[9] "dead body"
[10] "getted in my coobicle"
[11] "zer weren't no peoples in the store"

way to a guy passing by, who's solemnly carrying a whole suit in front of him, here — this is another camera — I'm showing my boo-ty to Ms. Cerberus, she gives me the numbers (in that moment I feverishly felt in my pocket, didn't I lose them? no, here they are), here I enter the fitting room, close the curtain, thoroughly pull-ing its end to the wall — another camera — I'm taking off my vest, reaching for the first hanger . . . stop! "Listen, what's this, do your cameras survey the fitting rooms?" He nodded his head in silence and continued handling the buttons. No, no, listen, but that's im-possible! privacy and all that, how can you watch fitting rooms? It was an order from above, too many thefts, people tear out the chips and put the things into their bags, do all that in the fitting rooms. A strict directive has been issued to put cameras into the fitting rooms too, and people from Britain have been sent for the surveil-lance, so here I am. They send us to Prague on business trips — for two weeks so that, according to the instructions, a prolonged stay in the city together with the observation of the camera materials of such delicate spaces as fitting rooms wouldn't lead to emotional in-volvement in the process of video surveillance, whose aim is security and prevention of theft of the goods, and also in order not to cause traumas to the psyche of the Bentham and Engels security staff by the necessity of an excessively long invasion into the intimate sphere of our esteemed shoppers. Naturally, it's all for their sake, for your sake, for the sake of our customers that we're doing this, so instead of happily sitting in my Battersea in the circle of family and friends, I'm forced now for the eleventh day in a row to observe a number of half-naked bodies and that has no doubt already left serious damage on my psyche, so I'll have to request a bonus to the salary and extra days off. Such simple-minded insolence disarmed me completely, I couldn't get one word out of my mouth, just watched the screen, where I was reaching for the dropped vest, froze at the sight of the barely visible gray spot next to the wall, straightened up, bent again to examine it properly, again straightened up, grasped the curtain to open it, didn't finish the movement and my hand fell down (I don't remember any of this!), stepped over the little gray stream, came out

of the cubicle, stood by the neighboring one—another camera—
tugged the curtain, knocked, moved my lips, carefully pulled the
fabric away, looked in, pulled it open, entered—another camera—
stood like frozen . . . stop . . . so you do have a camera there too, you
saw who killed her and how it all happened?

I am most sorry to say, no. The thing is, there's one cubicle in the
fitting-room area in which we're most strictly forbidden to switch
on the camera, without a special order from our management. The
customers entering that room have special cards of "Bentham and
Engels preferred customers," it's impossible to suspect them of an
attempt to cause material damage to our company, so we bashfully
drop our eyes, I mean cameras, and leave them alone with our outstanding goods. They have a right to that, don't they? It suddenly
seemed to me that he's mocking me. But no, it's those unpleasant
eyes all the time, the same irresolute mouth, the same gray face,
not a spark, not a shine, not a rustle, not a crunch. The guard was
speaking most seriously—it was impossible to doubt the assured-
ness and the loyalty of his words, it was more likely that I'd lost
my mind, not him, it's all right, it's got to be that way—people
steal things, it's necessary to survey the space, it's necessary for the
preferred clients to exist. Is it possible to trust nobody, nobody at
all? That's inhuman. True, simply inhuman. I began to feel ashamed
and I suddenly felt full of affection for this ugly man whose sense of
duty, order, and justice tore him away from his home and his local
pub and threw him here, into this godforsaken corner of Prague
life, into this stupid room, to these horrid gray screens with these
monstrous gray bodies on them. Who'd voluntarily watch strange
bellies, asses, chests? Wretched man, his face is all gray, it's obvious
he's got digestive problems, and he even eats dry stuff, washing away
the supermarket shit with Pepsi . . . Full of friendliness and sympa-
thy, I was about to ask him what we're supposed to be doing further,
should we call the police and can I go now when suddenly, jostling
its way through all these gestures of coming to peace with the reality
around me and with its indestructibly humanistic logic, a wholly
unpleasant question floated to the surface of my consciousness. And

I asked it. Tell me, there are cameras in the fitting rooms' corridor, let's see who entered *that* cubicle, and when?

The guard was watching me undisturbed. Still, I'm sure he too felt a kind of affection towards me, because suddenly he scratched his head and said: "In general, this is against the rules, but never mind, let's watch it." He turned to the panel again, pushed a few buttons and pointed with his finger at one of the screens. The corridor was perfectly empty, not a soul there. "This is ten minutes before you came in," he said over his shoulder with some ardor, "and this is fifteen minutes." From the fitting room that was destined to become mine, an old gentleman with an old lady came out, one after another, first she, then he, and moved towards the entrance in an Indian file, the man with his walking stick, the woman with a pile of things, part of which she left with the shop assistant, returned the numbers, he stood, waited for his wife and then they moved on — most likely to the cash registers. Nobody else. Nobody. I realized that it was the old man that I'd bumped into at the entrance to Bentham and Engels — the same, rosy-cheeked, smiling. "And when did the girl come into your special cubicle?" "Here, eighteen minutes before you." The blonde, hidden under a pile of clothes, pushed in between two awkwardly moving people in shorts coming out of the rooms, and disappeared from sight, only her hand appeared in a moment, pulling the curtain closed. That was it. She never came out again.

I suddenly felt so sick that I started thinking my Thai friends must've poisoned me but no, it passed fairly quickly, leaving weakness and sweat on my forehead. My mouth went dry and I asked the guard if he had some water. He took a plastic glass and poured some of his Pepsi there. The sickly-sweet, tepid liquid stood no chance of quenching my thirst but what it did was arm me for another level of communication with the lord of the cameras. After all, a murder happened, a person died, and he's sitting here, calm as ever, and pushing his buttons. Suspicions were crawling into my head, becoming more obtrusive, more specific, more paranoid with every passing second. Why isn't he calling the police? Why isn't he doing anything at all? Could it be a conspiracy? Against whom? Why was the blonde killed? Why didn't he even ask me what my name was? "Your name's Andrei," the guard suddenly responded to my thoughts, "you've been to Bentham about twenty times by now." Dreadful. How does he know? "You use a payment card with your name written on it. Our system automatically creates a file on every shopper, putting together the face from the video surveillance, their name, card number, and various other things. As soon as the shopper appears on this screen, the computer recognizes them and provides all the data—if we have them, of course. Alas, not all our shoppers are permanent, and so many of them leave without being recognized. But we're trying to establish cooperation with other store chains and I can tell you, we've been fairly successful; I daresay a universal database will've been created within a few years containing information on everybody who ever shopped in large European stores. As you certainly understand, we do all this not only to prevent thefts, but generally for our and your security. For the security of the society as a whole. We most willingly share this information with the counterintelligence, special services, and counterterrorist groups, and, it has to be noted, they appreciate it. Thanks only to this the authorities close their eyes to some minor violations of the law which we—when forced to!—permit ourselves; above all, of course, in your interests." The nausea returned; I didn't disbelieve my ears, no, I was just sitting there thinking I'm asleep, or rather that I'd died and ended up in hell. But he kept talking and talking, and my consciousness was catching bits and pieces of kind measured sentences . . . "responsibility that comes to us with doing business in former totalitarian countries . . . preventing minor robbery, we aren't as much interested in the prevention of financial loss as in the protection of the society's moral values . . . we are destined to stand invisible on the side of order and private property . . . centuries-old regulations blessed by the Church . . ." I fully realized that there's a madman next to me who somehow managed to smuggle cameras into the fitting rooms, a maniac, maybe of the sexual type, an abnormal lunatic, maybe even a murderer, why not, he sees everything, which means he can do everything, knowledge is power, isn't it, Mr. Bacon? "Oh no, what are you thinking," he responded to my mute outburst, "what murderer, I beg you. I never hurt a fly in my life. You Russians are prone to panic, Big Brother, KGB, surveillance, and all that. Nothing of the kind. Just a regular responsible running of a business in the current complicated situation." He switched on another screen in front of him, touched a few buttons with his finger and I saw myself, buying my Thai meal about an hour ago. "Here, look, ahead of you in the queue is standing Marcel Jirásek, a sociologist, he dedicates himself to issues of inequality in society. Postgrad at Charles University in Prague, PhD at the Central European University in Budapest, didn't finish his dissertation, a chronic freelancer. Returned to Prague a few years ago. A windbag. Hangs around with leftists. Stole pastry a few times in the Niels supermarket, but we pardoned him, didn't even retain him. We're not beasts, are we?" I felt as if lead was spreading through my nape. A tremendous exhaustion made me lean on the desk I was sitting at. I must have cut an amazing picture—sitting, with my head resting in my palm, listening like an attentive pupil, and the respectable man here is wasting his precious time to explain to me, simpleton, what life is about. I even became quite indifferent to the question of who killed Laura Palmer, sorry Laura Lyons, sorry damn, who killed her anyway, that hapless blonde from film noir, what they killed her for, and how they'll be punished. And the guard was still going on with his heavy nonsense. "Please pay attention to the other one, he works at the Superdebit bank, there's nothing about him, or just smallish things—used to download child porn sometimes, nothing more than that. We blocked his card, he then put a few thousand euros into a children's help fund, we unblocked it, since then he's been quiet, doing no harm—work, ice hockey on TV at night, beer, votes for the right wing, a regular citizen." In that moment my voice managed to cut through, but it was a weird, high, almost squeaky voice, not really mine: "Who's 'we'?" "Beg your pardon?" "Who's 'we'? Who's the 'we' who blocked this fellow's card?" "Aah . . . That's the Association for the Surveillance of Shoppers' Behavior, the fruit of the negotiations with the other store chains—and of course with the respective government authorities—that I told you about."

It dawned on me that now he'd start, in the same matter-of-fact tone of voice, kindly, full of information, to relate my own life to me, my arrival in Prague in the search of the "European spirit," of "culture," and lots of other things, about how I failed with all that, never wrote "the great European novel" full of historical and literary allusions, packed with philosophy and overgrown with a plot like Thomas Mann's, never properly learned the language of Jan Neruda and Bohumil Hrabal, didn't fall in love with Janáček's music, didn't write Kafka's biography, after which I started my methodical retreat from the center: from the center of Prague closer to the suburbs and from the "glorious cultural past" to the rough pop culture present, to the sophisticated misery of shopping malls, fast food, plastic life of mortgage-burdened people with the *Blesk* magazine under their arms. And about how I, in order to hide this failure from myself, thought to make a virtue out of necessity, to write a great European novel of contemporariness about misery, sophisticated and unsophisticated, create its megacatalogue, compendium, thesaurus. But how could he know that? Does he read people's minds? He does, remember, he was answering your mute questions. Yes, but now? What now? He's silent? Maybe got distracted? No, these androids never get distracted, that's what they're androids for. What android? He's a man. Androids don't drink Pepsi and don't eat bread rolls with cheese salad. And maybe they do. Who knows? Have you ever seen any? No. Shut up then. I'm not saying anything anyway. But why isn't he saying anything? The guard was sitting with his back towards me and watching his screens. His fingers were running along the buttons in the manner of a pianist, and scenes from the life of Bentham and Engels were flaring up here and there: a mother and daughter are feeling a cardigan, a shop assistant is scratching her back in discussion with a colleague, who's laying out the goods on the shelves, people are jamming in the fitting room, trying to hang something on a hook. I recognized my elderly couple—they were having trouble fitting in the narrow space, the wife was literally flattened against the wall, her husband was performing some really strange manipulations, not with the little hook but with the opposite wall, as if driving a screw into the wood. Then he froze, laying his cheek on it. He remained in this strange position for a few moments, then he drew back and again started to screw something into the wall. The old lady was calmly watching this handling, unmoving, only then did I notice that she was holding his stick in her hands and the clothes they'd brought were lying untouched in a pile on the bench.

"Christ, what are they doing?" "Can't you see—they're peeking in. Recording on a mini-camera." "What for?" "Andrei, you're an adult man, a writer so to speak, and yet you ask such childish questions. When older, people start having various wishes, including some rather strange ones. You mustn't consider old age a period of reconciliation and quiet burning down—there are some passions that flame up with a new strength, and some that only just appear. All in all, what's wrong with it if an elderly person spends a little while watching a beautiful young body? It won't hurt anyone; quite the contrary, it will give that person more strength to fight the aging. Who knows how many disorders and diseases they can avoid in this way, who knows ..." "Yes, but the girl ..." "And this is a real insult now, if not to say an offense! You're an almost regular customer of ours, you know how serious and how responsible an attitude our company has toward its work. And you dare suggest that we're violating moral statutes inherited from the founding fathers of Bentham and Engels, that we allow anybody to spy on our customers? How could you even think anything like that?" I was so taken aback by the insolence of this lunatic (yes, but *is* he a lunatic?) that I couldn't say a single word. He changed the well-played indignation into a calmer tone of voice, although the little precipitation, the little spell of cold after the unjust offense against his company— and against him personally—remained. "Of course, the young lady knows perfectly well she's being watched. She's one of our freelance contractors, Oksana Kochubei, from the beautiful Ukraine. It seems you were staying in Poltava a few years ago—did you by any chance

meet her there?" I gulped and shook my head. "By the way, there
are a lot of pretty young women in that country, always ready to
become a decoration of such a respected and venerable company as
ours. If you have a few more minutes to spare, I'll tell you the history of this service that we offer to the best of our customers. I can see
you wouldn't mind. Pour yourself more Pepsi, sit back comfortably,
c'mon, make yourself at home!

"So, a few years ago we noticed that there's a special category
of people visiting our store, usually elderly people, who aren't interested as much in clothes as in, so to speak, the whole market
paraphernalia. They were behaving somewhat strangely — they were
glancing, as if by mistake, into other people's fitting rooms, they
were even trying to create a system of mirrors in order to watch in
more detail some corners of the store space, and so on. That made
us think. You see, this kind of behavior isn't exactly in line with either our strict rules or with generally accepted social norms, or with
their age and position in life! Our first impetus was to discover these
people, reprimand them, or simply make the whole issue public
and strictly forbid them to visit our stores. After all, Bentham and
Engels has existed for over a hundred years and we're obligated to
watch over order and support traditional moral values, dammit!"
The guard livened up a little and even his grayness started to emit
something of a yellow hue that with a healthy dose of imagination could have passed off for a flush. He made an abrupt turn
in his chair before he continued with his narrative. "But on the
other hand, we're always on our customers' side. Attention to people
who visit us, not just a showy and indifferent attention, but a real
care — that's what's made the name of our company. And you've got
to accept the progress too! Of course, there were no such requests
addressed to our chain thirty years ago but we're always ready to
respond to the challenges of the times! All in all, you've got to build
on the fact that human life, oh yes, hu-man, is assigned the highest
value in our society, that's what distinguishes Western civilization
from all the others, backward, anti-humanistic, following obsolete
traditionalistic norms and customs. And they even want to push

their medieval values onto us! *Us*, who have carried the flame of humanism, lit by the ancient Greeks themselves! That will never happen, I promise you—solemnly and forever.

"That's when we decided to create a special service that would satisfy the somewhat specific requests of the best of our customers. No no, don't start thinking anything bad—it all happened and is happening within the limits of the law and according to the strictest demands of the best business conduct. We came up with a system of special fitting rooms where, based on the wishes of our permanent customers, came female and male freelancers, hired and trained by us for this purpose. The customers—and it needs to be said here that the cost of the Bentham and Engels special card is rather substantial and you need recommendations from influential and respected people, you understand, we cannot let these issues put our reputation in danger—so these customers were taking the neighboring rooms and could closely observe the most precious moments. Later we allowed them to use cameras, mini-camcorders and other technological devices. You know, it was simply amazing to see how old people, who never dreamed of catching up with technological progress again, of controlling gadgets and devices of the third millennium, were suddenly getting the knack of the most contemporary little machines! God, many of them were happy as children when they succeeded in recording a small video clip and then uploaded it to our website!"

I felt like I had been hit by electric current. "What website now?" "Don't you understand? Do you think we could allow anybody to upload video clips of certain delicate content, so to speak, somewhere out there? On YouTube or Porn.com? We understand perfectly that publication would be fatal for us and our customers alike! And the girls? Have you thought about them? Somebody sees how a promising PhD student of the faculty of biology takes off her clothes in front of the eyes of millions of people? Her career would be ruined forever—and this country that experienced firsthand all the humiliation of being ruled by another state, of totalitarian regime, foreign occupation, and, between us, the pernicious influence of the transatlantic globalization, this country needs its own scientists, managers, and tutors. And who are we to deprive them — and the whole country — of their future with a single step? Never!" He was so yellow now that I was ready to believe that in some human beings, bile stands for blood. The guard performed two turns on his chair, had a gulp straight from the bottle and continued. "Yes, we created our own website where it's possible to upload video clips, shot by our talented customers, and believe me, we didn't spare means to ensure its perfect protection. Of course, I won't give you the address, but even if you found it somehow, you wouldn't get in. Of course, should you buy our special card . . . To be honest, I've come to like you, and I could have a word with the management so that they'd allow you to become its owner — regardless of some strange little things in your biography, youthful indiscretions, so to speak, but let's be fair, who was completely discrete in their youth? So? Think about it. My proposal is valid until the end of our conversation. But let us return to our story. There's little left to tell. The special program of Bentham and Engels has proved to be extraordinarily successful; more than that, we've been able to inform the government authorities about it as a socially beneficial project and even receive some tax relief in connection with it. Not bad when the government supports social initiatives, eh? Especially when it's business going hand in hand with society, and the government blesses their union. That is, dammit, the core of democracy — not that which the Yanks are trying to force upon us but ours, European, based on the millennia of high culture and developed civilization." From yellow he started turning into plain green, I didn't know where to hide, maybe I should run? But he'll shoot me . . . having noticed that my eyes stopped at his gun case, the guard nodded silently. Yes. He'll shoot. But it was impossible to stay there longer, I was literally dying from this filth unchained that his damned mouth was spouting at me. Simply for the sake of stopping him, I asked quietly: "And the girl?"

"Oksana? Oh yes. A venerable German couple who'd settled in Prague a few years before came to like our Poltavian beauty. So much so that their mutual relations went somewhat beyond the line set by our regulations, which, believe me, are very, very strict. They were inviting her home, recording video clips, doing something else too—but here I fall silent! We're always on guard for our customers' private lives. All in all, there was a nasty plot coming along—either it was them uploading some video to a publicly accessible site or it was her blackmailing them, threatening to make their fine (especially the fine!) diversions the property of the Worldwide Cobweb. In the end, all this started to exert a rather intense pressure on our elderly couple and even to threaten their health. Could we stand aloof?" "And you . . ." "No no, never! We're simply a chain store, we make the wishes of our customers happen, we create the best possible conditions for it, but no more! Who if not us stands on the side of the law?" "That means, you?" "All we did was give two deserving, well-respected members of society a chance to punish an unwise creature upon whom they'd poured favors, but who'd shown monstrous ungratefulness. We asked Oksana to come to a usual video session in the special fitting-room, having provided our dear customers with the option to use a narrow blade instead of the video camera, hidden in that wondrous stick that you undoubtedly haven't failed to notice. We didn't even have to drill a new hole in the dividing wall, all they had to do was take the camera out, strike the right blow, then put the camera back in again, I'm only afraid that this video will hardly find a place for itself on our site. But it will certainly embellish the collection of our couple. What could be more thrilling than the moment of death of a beautiful, young, half-naked being? It's worth all your ancient Greek tragedies together . . ."

I heard his last words from afar, in the corridor, on the way, I mean—on the run. Let him shoot, the bastard, let him shoot. Within moments I reached the exit from the corridor, kicked the door open, jumped out into the store and froze. It was full. People were walking along the shelves, feeling the clothes, women in uniforms were crawling among them and returning order to the chaotic heaps of clothes; a long hanger on wheels rode by me, pushed by a long-haired young man with tattoos on his neck. He may have been the only one to notice my entrée, and he cast me a furtive glance of serious disapproval. I couldn't catch my breath, after all, he won't chase me here, he won't kill me with all the people around, right? Totally right. And then, what can I do? Where should I go? Who should I call for help? I'd spent about an hour in the room with the screens, the body should've been long found during that time. But why isn't the store closed then? Where are the police? The camera flashes? Where are specialists in white coats? And the press people? I carefully walked among the racks and hangers for a few minutes, pretending to be highly interested in the new collection of Bentham clothes. Nothing. No thing. There was one last thing to do—go to the crime scene and see for myself. I grasped a T-shirt and went to the fitting-room area. Nodding to the scowling lady at the entrance, I got a number from her and headed for the same room where it had all started. Thank God, it was empty and what's more, there were the exact same T-shirts I'd brought in here an hour ago. I pulled the curtain closed and kneeled down. No traces of blood, none at all. I examined every scratch on the yellow lino, nothing. All right now, there's still the wall. I examined the plastic surface with the thoroughness of a money-changer at an Istanbul market, but discovered no holes, no cameras, no drops of blood. Finally, I kneeled down again and looked under the wall into the neighboring cubicle. There were two bare feet standing there. Two hands appeared, brought a pair of jeans to the feet, one foot rose and entered the jean. Here it was, it came out of the blue fabric, rested on the floor and the other foot moved in the same direction as the first one. I came out of the cubicle, and glanced, as if by accident, in the direction of the imperfectly closed curtain. My gaze met with a pair of black eyes—from inside, a naked arm appeared and angrily pulled the curtain to the end. And I headed for the exit, returned the three numbers to the shop assistant, left two T-shirts with her, came up to the register, paid for the purchase, observed how the skillful cashier tears the chip away from the fabric, said "*Děkuji*,"[12] took the company bag with the gorgeous logo of Bentham and Engels, and left.

---

[12] "Thank you."

Amadeus

This is the picture: snowy courtyard of a former bishop's palace, currently used as a museum. Actually, not a courtyard, just an enclosed garden, and thanks to baroque masters' vainglorious endeavors, it's full of big-butted sculptures, paths, various plants, and even a small stream, with a chubby stone boy in the middle, spouting water from his little weenie. He pees here in the spring, summer, and at the beginning of autumn; but now it's winter in the courtyard, there are no leaves, no fountain, and no visitors, there's nobody to enjoy the sight of the half-frozen stream, with the grayish ice floating in the black water. But there are people here, or, rather, there were, quite recently: somebody walked there and back, from the massive curved door opening onto the main alley of the courtyard to the furthest wall, embellished by a gallery that used to be draped with plush, but all that remains now is a skinny wooden frame, interwoven with dry, thin plush tentacles, unpleasant to look at. Through all that a wall can be seen, yellow and covered in wet spots; cracks and peeled-off plaster constitute its main decoration. Footprints lead straight to the gallery and then back to the door; they're printed clearly in the snow, untouched since last night, nobody comes here at this time of year, nobody drops in. Their appearance itself is strange but what's even stranger and more incomprehensible, is something else: in the middle of the courtyard the two pairs of feet going together turn into one pair that serenely heads for the gallery, turns around and, as if nothing happened, comes back. The other pair is suddenly cut off on the way there, without a reason or even an excuse, just so: here's somebody walking next to the person number one, maybe they went in silence or maybe they were talking, calmly or heatedly, we don't know that, and suddenly—the person is no more. Strange thing, strange and unfathomable.

* * *

The courtyard looked desolate from the museum window as is proper at a place which great style has left, abandoning all its material

paraphernalia, and those now continue to live on in a wholly different world—shabby and worn down, but still heavily protected,
which adds a particularly hopeless air to the loneliness of the stone
and iron, twisted, wrought, united into strange constructions for
the glory of ideas that the descendants won't understand. There were
a lot of footprints in the snow, they were roaming around without
crossing the main line: the chain of four parallel footprints, later
of two, leading there and back. Turning away from the window,
I asked the first and most important question: "So, did you tell
them?" Sergey Morvid merrily nodded his big head, his eyes cheerful, lively, and frightened. The police had only just left him alone,
they were now wandering around the museum, which was closed
for this reason, its staff were questioned and then sent home, the
entrance was barred with a striped band and by a sluggish giant
wearing a uniform, with a big handgun stuck in too small a holster
(how did he manage to fit it in? Or is all of it together, the gun and
the leather case, a model, a toy, a scarecrow for the nervous Prague
pickpockets and grim junkies, destroyed by cheap crap?). Neither
my level of insolence nor my beastly Czech would've been adequate
for me to enter into an interesting conversation with a policeman
about big handguns and small holsters (something almost divine
rings in this word, doesn't it: *holster*, a rhyme for *apostle*); I should be
glad he let me in at all—me, a foreigner and journalist, and therefore doubly dangerous and suspicious. Saying, Mr. Morvid doesn't
have a lawyer, so he asked a friend to come and offer him both
moral support and advice in this strange situation he cannot begin
to understand. Had there been a real offense, robbery, rape, murder,
nobody would've let in such a villain as me but here . . . What's there
to investigate when there's nothing: just the footprints and fables
of a museum guy, who's certainly nuts, about how he was walking
in the courtyard with a crazy guest from Russia and how, halfway
through an unhurried discussion about divine retribution and its
falling upon the heads of sinners, one of the participants suddenly
disappeared, dissolved in the damp air of the Prague Castle—or was
by the wave of the Lord's hand instantly taken away in an unknown

direction, hell or heaven, it's impossible to say which. "So was it heaven or hell? What do you think?" Morvid scratched his chin with his miniature monkey-like hand and blurted out: "Heaven!" "Why so, my dear Sergey? He was . . . I mean he *is* . . . either way, he's a blasphemer?" "Apophatically, Andrei, apophatically. These days you don't have many people who'd think about God. I don't mean take His name in vain or in times of need, but *think*. Be it in an ill way, without any preparation or skill for it, but *think*. Laika thought." "In the past tense?" "Of course, my dearest Andrei! He doesn't think now, he *sees!*" It was difficult to object to this exaltation, born of a long habit of homemade sweet-and-sour theologizing mixed with a quiet hysterics caused by the fantastic event. Go to Lourdes and try to give the ill a scientific lecture on remission.

"So what, did he disappear?" "He did!" shouted Morvid in rapture, his eyes glistening, his hands playing with the museum leaflets. A fidgety police specialist with a gigantic bag is wandering around the courtyard. He stops. Takes a camera out of the bag. Snaps. Puts the camera back in. Wanders around again. "Did you tell them everything?" "Of course! Everything they wanted to know." "As in, not everything?" "Andrei, tell me, why would the police need to know about the concept of awakened God?" "What God?" "Awakened. Woken up from a sleep. Disturbed. Emerged from a coma."

This was how Morvid described the whole thing. Laika, having arrived in Prague on an early train, immediately went to the museum, as he'd agreed with Sergey, who on this special occasion crept to work at seven thirty in the morning. The idea was that they'd spend the whole day together in a theological dispute, after which the artist would take the Moscow-bound train late at night and go back home. Morvid would go home too, but much closer, into his small apartment not far from the Strahov Monastery, about half-an-hour's walk from the former bishop's palace. Sergey was counting down the years left to his retirement so that he could ride on the tram free of charge; for now, the modest salary made him exercise his legs and heart on the magnificent cobblestones of the Hradčany district every working day. Once, at the height of the January black ice, he slipped and fell down so badly that he then spent ages in hospitals, where his broken legs were being put together, glued together and grown back together. Then it took Morvid a long time to learn how to walk anew; the doctors advised him to use ski poles, so that's how he was moving about Hradčany now—a skier without skis, a shoe-nonmaker with huge boots that the doctors had prescribed him because of the heavy damage to his legs, the poles moving back and forth, knocking on the pavement. A look to make saints laugh—but Sergey would never let those be offended. Some time before we knew each other, that is before I moved to Prague, he even wrote up something of a treatise about the Czech saints. Didn't manage to have it published but I got a home-printed copy of this masterpiece at our first meeting in autumn 2001—that precisely was how Morvid advised me to start my studies of the local life. Not from the dumplings, beer, foreigners' police department, and discussions about President Havel's second marriage, but from the saints of the Czech lands (and of Moravia alike). I didn't conquer his work but I did have a look: the author was basing it on a concept, created by himself, of a special gently malicious type of the Slavic holiness; all of his heroes possessed, as the author put it, "kind cunning," which was the result of the transitional position of the Czech nation between the warlike eastern Slavs and no less cruel and rough Germans. None of my arguments about, as it seemed to me, true personal characteristics of the local inhabitants were having any influence on Morvid; he took it so far as to believe the Czechs played ice hockey in a gentle and cunning way. To discuss the kind cunning of Jaromír Jágr was more than I was capable of.

And so, here I am, sitting in his office like hundreds of times before; by the entrance door stand the legendary ski poles, on the rug stand the equally legendary boots four sizes larger than Morvid's feet. It's them that are printed out there, in the snow, next to the mystically vanishing footprints of the blasphemous Russian artist who'd been punished (or rewarded) by the Lord Himself. "And how did you get that idea at all? What theological disputes? Or even duels—that's what you called it . . ." "Andrei, and how else do you imagine a discussion about God's wrath and retribution? What's it supposed to look like? Filthy posts in LiveJournal?" Morvid moved here immediately after the notorious shelling of the White House in Moscow, learned the local language perfectly, but still, strangely, kept using his Russian. That is, not even kept; he jumped, fluttered, galloped, emptied himself, reproduced himself by division with his mother tongue that had fallen in a perfectly whorish position in the modern world, offering itself to everybody right and left: the merry American, the gold-toothed Mongolian, the distilled auditor, and even the Tajik caretaker. We've been enjoying the fruits of lexical fornication for about twenty years and together with us — the emigrant of theology, Czechophile, and connoisseur of saints, Sergey Morvid.

"Yes, LiveJournal . . . But, Sergey, wasn't that where you bumped into Laika for the first time?" "Andrei, dear, I beg you, what nonsense is this now? Are you saying that if you meet an interesting partner for discussion in a dirty alehouse, you shouldn't go beyond its pissed boundaries for anything in the world?" I liked the "pissed boundaries"; there was something Jesuit, Latin, Mercatorian about it. Isn't he a Catholic, by the way? Hardly. The more so that the ascended (descended) Laika, they say, was friends with the author of the work that caused an outcry in its time, *Obossany pistolet*,[13] which Morvid knew well — it was him who let me read this work of the cheeky artistic genius, who'd defaced Kazimir Malevich's colorful squares. A year in a Dutch prison he got for it . . . Some time ago, in the half-starved Russian years, it would've seemed to me that's not exactly a punishment . . . As for Laika, he didn't write books. Or paint pictures, God be praised. First he barked, and he did it so credibly that dogs were gathering when he did and started a yapping shootout with him. How Boris Mitrich-Korovin — who only later received his sweet doggy nickname — did this, is hard to understand. Cynologists shrugged their shoulders, specialists babbled something or other about certain wavelengths with which Laika's voice resonated, but nobody was able to find out for sure. One way or another, Laika kicked off his career with real zeal, standing on his hind legs

[13] Pissed Handgun

and with his head proudly tilted back: as soon as a year later he was touring around with a pack of dogs performing the anthem of the Soviet Union and "God Save the Tsar." The dog-and-bitch band was desperately out of tune, but the look of it was unforgettable. The main role in the success of the Dog Anthem performance was played by communists and monarchists who put up wild protests, creating open letters demanding an exemplary punishment. Laika also got beaten up in a Moscow passageway but not too much, which gave the audience a reason to doubt the authenticity of the incident. The artist beat himself up, right. The doubts made sense: the thing was that nobody ever saw Laika. At the performances, he was always wearing an overalls made of dog skins, and a mask depicting a werewolf; his voice wasn't heard either because the artist didn't speak, he barked. In Austria, Laika was known as X-Mongrel, the British named him Russian Banksy. Anyway, the doggy music show became boring pretty quickly; furthermore, anybody could tear the dog skin from his trembling body or shout: "Laika, take off the mask!" To make a long story short, he disappeared.

Not altogether, of course. All Laika did was simply move, having made for himself an online kennel. There he began the main project of his life, called *Dear God, Punish Me!* Laika was exercising in blasphemy, posting various nasty pictures that would've been punishable not only by thunder and heavenly fire but also very simply in accordance with the criminal law. Pedophilia, little jokes about the victims of the Holocaust and the GULAG, appeals to overthrow the authorities—all this mixed with juicy anticlericalism and dishonoring of Him above. Laika's blog was attacked by Orthodox and liberal hackers, it was shut down by grim prosecutors of Saransk and Magnitogorsk cities (and Moscow prosecutors issued an arrest warrant straight away), all in vain; the Kennel (as he called his internet bunker) kept coming back to life all the time in various places; the diligent warrior with the World Order and the Divine Order was regularly posting documents proving how he, wretched and unloved, was being pursued by everybody around; then he again took up the atrocities. The public were in turns mocking him, taking offense, and applauding—anything but forgetting the son of a bitch. And he was enjoying the power over people's minds and imaginations, and once a month he sent to God a detailed electronic list of his heroic deeds, always adding at the end: "Well, dear God, punish me!" And now my friend Morvid here was persuading me that He had punished him. Or at least taken notice.

Normally quiet Sergey immediately got pulled into the whole story. At first he was honestly writing comments to Laika's offensive posts, and later created a special blog, where he entered into a theological dispute with the artist. Oh, no, he didn't subject the blasphemer's opinions to rough moral judgment, didn't argue with him about humanism or even common sense, didn't persuade, didn't curse, didn't yap. No. Morvid came as an interpreter, translator of God—only not of the Word of God, but the absence of the Word. Why the Highest One is silent when He—and His people—are ridiculed by a half-illiterate, primitive, stupid, cynical swine, stinking ugly bitch Laika? Sergey calmly and logically offered him an explanation; everything was as it should be: the jester's raging, the tsar's smiling into his beard and not saying anything. The more hysterical the clown's frenzy, the more reasonable the theologian's argumentation. Finally Laika, beside himself with fury, announced that he'd beat Morvid black and blue. Sergey's reaction to this proposal was perfectly cordial: come to Prague, we'll meet, we'll talk. And so they did.

Having drunk some tea and more or less calmed Sergey down, I set out for editorial—to put together the material about what had happened. The local expat English-language newspaper had no business dealing with Dostoyevskian contentions of former Russians, but the story about the footprints in the snow was eagerly accepted. So, two plots were created. One, Baskervillian, about the disappearance of the other pair of feet. The other one, Leskovian, about a psychopathic blasphemer and a calm saint. I alone knew about the third one, the Chestertonian, about the theology duel with the violent (volant?) outcome.

The issue was swept under the carpet rather quickly; or, it swept *itself*, based on the fact that the injured party (or, the disappeared party—we don't know whether Laika was *injured* in the process of vanishing) was never seen by anybody. The border control confirmed that a citizen of the Russian Federation of the surname "Mitrich-Korovin" did enter the territory of the Czech Republic on a train the night preceding the fatal discussion. He did not leave the country. Nobody missed Laika in Russia, understandably, and the internet mockers, certain that the artist went into hiding while working on another prank, refocused on some scandalous lexicographer and his cohort. Timur, the self-appointed linguist, was producing one after another dictionaries, dedicated to the culinary vocabulary of the Russian language, and his retinue were attacking the customers of famous Moscow restaurants, tying them up, and sticking into the mouths of the bourgeoisie pages torn out of the immortal works of their black-bearded guru. The project was called *Quail the Gour-met*. One of the victims didn't survive the mockery and died on the spot in the hands of the art-revolutionaries. The lexicographic war ended in trials, hurried escapes abroad, warrants from Interpol, and a large-scale international discussion about how far contemporary art is allowed to go. As usual, no conclusion was arrived at. Who'd remember some poor blasphemous dog? As for the Czech police, for them, of course, the absence of a person meant there was no problem to solve. And who ever saw this guy? Who looked for him?

Morvid did look for him. He kept sending letters to the police directorate, went on audiences to the deputy minister of the interior, and made his journalistic acquaintances write articles about the strange, incomprehensible disappearance of the insolent blasphemer. All in vain. In the end, the authorities hinted that should Mr. Morvid stubbornly persist in his actions, they should be forced to question the state of his mind as well as examine the issue of whether such an exalted (although very knowledgeable, cultured, and professional) person should be working at a position which requires him daily to deal with the treasures of Czech painting. Maybe he shouldn't. Sergey fell silent, withdrew, almost stopped calling. He didn't believe that anybody believed his version of the story of

Laika's disappearance; to tell the truth, I didn't quite believe that I believed it myself.

A year passed. It was winter again, and there was snow—a thing not all that frequent in this region, but almost obligatory in recent years, global warming, cooling, devil knows them. I was making my way through the wondrously slippery square between the Loreta cloister and the ministry of foreign affairs; the tourists around were staggering, falling, guffawing (Italians), swearing (Russians). It was fun and it was dreadful to move one's feet carefully from one cobblestone covered in ice to another, especially on the sloping pavement; to cut a long story short, when I fell down and was on all fours, musing about which hand was supposed to come off the ground first, Sergey's gigantic boots suddenly entered my vision and stopped. He was standing above me, with ski poles in his hands, a kind and awkward smile on his lips, above his head was a strangely blue sky, embellished by allegorical, curly clouds. "I'm sorry for not giving you a hand—but I'd fall myself!" "No worries," I was back on my two feet by now, shaking the snow off, fixing the backpack on my back, greeting my good friend, "I can do it. Haven't seen you for ages! What's your news?"

There was a lot of news, a lot—almost five hundred pages of the second Morvid treatise—this time not about the Czech saints but about the source of all holiness, about God. Sergey had settled the score with the story of Laika's disappearance, and with Laika himself, who now couldn't respond to anything. And there was a lot to tell him, a lot to bark out! Not content with banal judgments about the apophatic proof of God's existence, Morvid suggested a wholly unimaginable treatment of the issue: he called the blasphemer "saint," who was with his insults attempting to "awaken God from His sleep." "You wouldn't start telling off a hoodlum who slapped an old man lying in coma, if the man magically woke up as a result? Quite the contrary. Endless will be the gratefulness. The artist Laika set as his goal to wake up God, who had stopped granting attention to this world. And he succeeded. God woke up and took Laika, like He took the saints when their lives, full of work, ended." All this I read later, in the evening and during the following several evenings; and then we sat down together in a tearoom in Neruda Street, with a certificate hanging behind Morvid's back about how here, in this building, Miloš Forman had shot some scene or other of *Amadeus*. I was sipping tepid gyokuro, Sergey was fighting his way through some complicated ayurvedic drink, a group of cheerful Russians fell into the café, with cameras, small bags, guides, all wrapped in carefully tied "casual" scarves of bright colors, three girls, two boys. One of the boys immediately went to search for a bathroom, made a mistake, instead of the bathroom opened a door into some staff room, awkwardly excused himself, snagged on a chair, dropped something . . . "Borya, have you gone mad!" shouted one of the ladies with rosy cheeks, her black eyes like olives, unruly curls falling out from under a knitted Tibetan cap. Morvid sighed. "I don't want to rush you but I'd really appreciate it if you could read that book I gave you. You understand, after what happened a year ago, I can't return to my previous life. I'm lonely. As if I'd lost myself." I had my doubts regarding the sincerity of his words, but upon noticing the serious, almost martyred look of him, I realized he wasn't exaggerating.

The treatise was dedicated to "B. M.-K." and was Morvid's masterpiece. About four hundred years ago, in the baroque Prague, it would have been examined, reprinted, passed from hand to hand, from library to library, extolled and reviled. Nobody needed it now, myself included. I don't know about the Highest One, but the God of the theology genre wasn't sleeping—he'd long been lying in his grave, giving no hints of resurrection. But I couldn't get out of my mind this Laika story; and crucial was not the question *where* the blasphemer had disappeared and not even *whether* he'd disappeared at all, but something completely different: has the main and only witness of the event, Sergey, taken leave of his senses? In my mind, I was analyzing that discussion we'd had together, when I rushed to his office immediately after he asked me to, how I was questioning him, who was taken aback, frightened and exalted, how he was staring at the courtyard, at the chains of footprints in the snow, how he turned his look at the room, the writing desk with an old-fashioned computer, the ski poles and the boots in the corner, next to them a black bag, darkened with dampness, a funny coffee table from the "normalization" era of the seventies, two cups, a teapot, carefully wrapped in a perfectly vintage towel with an embroidery, almost an ancient Slavic ritual cloth, a very Soviet sandwich with butter and cheese, which the nervous theologian is offering to share with me, excuse me Andrei, I never expect anybody, always bring food only for myself alone but it's too much for me, too much, I actually don't feel like eating . . . God, what nonsense.

Unlike in 2001, I couldn't avoid discussing Morvid's opus this time; even the treatise itself was of a wholly different type and quality, let alone the conditions and motives of its writing. I had to meet with Sergey; as soon as I understood that, I started the preparations: knowing the museum-ish, bibliographic character of my friend, I had to be fully armed—to speak persuasively, to have all the facts and versions in my hands, to interpret seriously, logically, and, after all, irrefutably. I did my best. After (and often instead of) my work I browsed Russian forums and blogs and studied the infamous biography of Boris Mitrich-Korovin aka Laika, his howling, barking, and teeth-grinding, his despicable provocateurship, his heavy schizophrenia, which, I'm sure, had determined his destiny from its start, covered in Soviet fog, to the uncomely end. Finally, I was ready. Called him. Agreed to meet in the same tearoom as before. It's strange they haven't named the place Amadeus.

Ayurvedic tea. Gyokuro. Everything exactly like two weeks ago, only there are no Russian tourists this time, nobody takes the staff room for the lavatory. "Boris . . ." Morvid tore his eyes away from the cloudy cinnamon-like liquid in his cup and gave me a strange look. "What?"

"You remember, how the last time there were Russians here, shouting loudly . . ."

"Oh, yes. So, the book? Do you like it?"

"Wonderful, Sergey, wonderful. You, how they'd say nowadays in Russia, closed the issue. There's nothing more to say. The truth's there, disclosed in all its light. Black light."

"Why black? You aren't accusing me of Gnosticism, are you?"

"No, how could I ... Although there is something Gnostic about this whole story ... No. It's not Gnosticism but immeasurable, monstrous, unchained vanity."

"...?"

"So, yes, of course, vanity, and what else? A quiet life during the last breath of the socialist regime, wretchedness of a provincial associate professor in Gaidar's Russia, what else? ... Escape to the pitiful Czech land, to the museum, strangers around, strange books, all strange, cold, making no sense. All that's left is to weave together fairytales about the Czech holiness ... More tea?"

"No-no, I still have some, thank you! So, what else?"

"Yes ... And then suddenly, thanks be to you, God of Silicon Valley, some internet appears there, Russian drivel, forums, blogs ... Gives unlimited possibilities to preach, create, make up things ... You begged somebody there in Russia to act the dog?"

"Andrei, you're a skeptic, and such are not to understand the whole greatness and power of the Lord, be it a regional and silicone one. Who ever saw my Laika in person? And his dogs? Nobody. His performances were written about, true; even some video appeared but, you understand yourself, to find a few minutes of doggy video on the internet and add a different sound to it ... Well, I mean ..."

"Damn, you're even smarter ... And I naïvely thought about collaborants, accomplices, assistants ... But it doesn't matter anymore. Then your Laika got listed as a blasphemer and villain. What for?"

"Andrei, you read my book! Or didn't read it again? No? Yes?"

"All right, got it. To awaken God from His sleep. More precisely, to awaken the most esteemed public from its sleep with regards to God. A beautiful and most noble goal ..."

"And what is it that you don't like about it?"

"The lies, dear Morvid, the lies. The sophisticated, hysterical, creative lies. No, not theology—the lies of a schizophrenic. It was all for the sake of power, and not for God, was it? You made up a son of a bitch, then silenced him, in the same way silencing the Highest

One, and then wrote a treatise about it, didn't you?" Morvid was silent. He wasn't disturbed. Or upset. He was rejoicing.

"Well, and then you reached the finale, a true Chestertonian finale, theology together with the disappearance of a person in the middle of a city—that's typical Gilbert Keith. Your other passport came handy, the one in your real name?"

"First, Andrei, my first passport."

"Well yes, Boris. That's what I mean. The first. Just don't tremble at the sound of this name. Aren't there enough Borises?"

"Andrei, my dear, I knew I'd be caught on this."

"And the other, the wet pair of boots in the bag? And only one sandwich for two people, for yourself and—don't get upset—*Boris*? You were meeting him at the station? Wouldn't you feed the blasphemer?"

"Mea culpa. Several blunders. But the plan was carried out! It all succeeded!" Cunning flamed up again in his look, but this time it was heavy, evil, hopeless, nothing besides it, except the wish to lie, just for the sake of it, to mystify everything, his own life, another life, life in general, theology, criminalistics, everything. There's nothing except the lie, that endless winking at oneself in the mirror that reflects in the mirror opposite, and so on, until everything in this world becomes an eternal, evil, cunning sneer, hopeless smirk of the specter of Communism, Hirst's grinning skull, covered in gritted brilliants. "Well, in fact, Gnosticism, yes."

"You think so?" I heard a bashful hope in his voice, no, don't give any hints on the fulfilling of wishes, plans, etc., none, or else cunning again, that holiness for the wretched. "I'll pay for it. The tea."

"You're very kind, Andrei . . ."

"You think so?"

We were slowly making our way up the Neruda Street, that is, I was making my way, and Morvid was crawling along, swinging his poles. People were backing away awkwardly, only children were giggling, but from afar, at a safe distance. "If you dress your poles in those shoes, there'll be three of us, not two. Did you practice for a long time? The footprints looked very real."

"I'm a serious person, Andrei. Of course. A few months. Traveled to Russia. Bought two pairs. Threw away one of them later, they were falling off the pole baskets. Sprinkled sand on the floor at home, learned, studied the prints. I'd say I was successful!"

"It was splendid, just splendid. And further, the way I imagine it? You came to the museum before anybody else, put the boots on the poles, walked with them halfway through the courtyard, then took the poles into one hand, shoes into the other, to the wall, then back, and no more Laika? Dissolved in thin air? Gone with the wind?" Morvid cut a nice look: flushed, either from the walk or from the satisfaction, or from God knows what. No, not nice, of course not, strange, just strange; it was joy but joy that had no relationship whatsoever to me, to the others, to the human race. It was as if he were giving thanks to a God unknown to me, and I was present somewhat awkwardly, a stranger to his joys and games ... And anyway, I'm tired and it's time to go home. We came out to the square, in the middle of it stands a plague column, behind us and on the left is a church, turned into a hotel, kiosks selling trifles, a café for idlers. A gray, rag-like sky. Freezing, freezing to the bone. "Well anyway, I've got to go. Thank you, Andrei, for reading my book to the end. You understood almost everything truthfully, bravo." He took both the poles in one hand and held the other out to me. Oh my God, of course! "Listen, you don't need those!"

"What don't I need?"

"The poles. Ski poles."

"Well, no, I don't. So what?"

"So why have you been dragging them along for ten years? Who do you want to fool?"

"No, Andrei, I shouldn't have praised you. You haven't understood anything. Goodbye."

He hardly ever changed them during all the years, those ski poles. Their points had worn down against the Prague cobblestones. The baskets were all damaged and badly scratched. The handgrips were disfigured, the straps had long gone nobody knows where. I took a close look at them while I was waiting for the investigator the next day, in the little courtyard of the former bishop's palace, in the shallow, thawing snow. The scared museum workers were crowding behind a huge glass door, I could see their vague, limp gestures, gray faces, soundless sentences. Two chains of footprints were leading from the door; in the middle of the courtyard the two pairs of feet turn into one pair that serenely heads for the gallery, turns around and, as if nothing happened, comes back. The other pair is suddenly cut off on the way there, without a reason or even an excuse, just so: here's somebody walking next to the person number one, maybe they went in silence or maybe they were talking, calmly or heatedly, we don't know that, and suddenly — the person is no more. Strange thing, strange and unfathomable. But there's something else, even stranger. Next to the door, next to the trash can, lies a pair of ski poles. Next to them, leaning on the wall, sits their owner, Sergey Morvid, he's mort, excuse me, he's dead. Rigor mortis has set in. His head is drooping in an ugly way with the unnaturally extended neck, from which hangs a piece of a cord. Another piece is tied to the gorgeous, baroque-style, copper door handle. Morvid's legs are stretched out. If you wish, you can compare the pattern of the soles of his huge boots with the footprints in the snow, those that walked there and back. As for the other pair, it's lying, hurriedly stuck into the wet black bag, in the trash can. I know it, but won't tell anybody.

The Last Film of Vlasta S.

We've got to walk up two steps, passing on our right the bar counter of a blurred, dim bluish-greenish color, and the brightly lit shelves full of bottles, seeing immediately that for instance, brandy enjoys a much lower demand than rum or Jameson; in the corner on the left stands a table; just a year ago it was occupied for most of the time by a busy, rather boorish, couple; at first sight they looked like they'd just got out of bed after enjoying the monotonous joys of copulation, with both his and her lips a little swollen, as if bitten in a grim paroxysm just a second ago; I always thought them to be country people who'd made it as far as estate agents or even small bank clerks, until I accidentally ran into them at the airport; on their backs were hanging a violin case (his) and a cello case (hers); afterwards during the long evenings in the Medina café I observed their long fingers, the graceful movements when he held up a match to her cigarette, studied their alcohol assortment (cocktails—hers, beer—his); to make a long story short, if we pass the corner table on our left where the string duet for some reason or other haven't sat for a long time, preferring the table in the middle of the small lounge, and pass inside into the short corridor, which creates an even shorter branch to the storage room on the left, where (if the light's on) you can always see the edge of a case of Coke or the crumpled side of a metal beer barrel, on the right, one after another, are the doors into the ladies' and gentlemen's rooms and, finally, the corridor ends in the kitchen. Its door is open (almost) all the time, the kitchen closes very late, after midnight and when it's clear that none of the patrons who're staying late is going to get an idea of a midnight snack. The door's now standing wide open, we can see the fridge, the microwave on the windowsill, on top of it baguettes, cut loaves of bread for toast, and some other food, waiting to be un-packed. We can't see anything else, because the kitchen makes an L with respect to the corridor, and in order to see the better part of the space, you've got to go in and look right. There's a sink, cupboards with plates hanging on the wall, orderly hung towels, and a mur-

muring dishwasher. The perfect order is interrupted only by a girl lying on the floor, the look of her glassy eyes is directed sideways, her head faces away from the body. The blood flowing from her slit throat has made a large scarlet puddle, some kind of halo around her light hair strewn about.

We grouped in the narrow wooden opening and silently looked at the only too cinematic scene. The silence was disturbed only by the rustling of the dishwasher as it went from the washing to the drying stage. Markéta, who'd cried out so loudly a minute ago that all of the five or six people who were having their last Friday drink immediately ran to the kitchen, wasn't sobbing, but her face with wide cheekbones was glistening with tears. "Call the police," I heard somebody say behind me; the violinist pushed past me back to the corridor and within a moment I heard his quiet shaking tenor. I never thought that this well-built young man with a fat neck and watery eyes would speak in the voice of Vertinsky. I turned to Markéta. "Close the door to the café. Don't let anybody in or out." She nodded and, casting a quick glance at the dead girl, vanished behind my back. A tall Englishman (a couple of whiskies and a liter of beer per evening, long manicured fingers, a friend of the string players, a man who's a spitting image of Reinhold from *Berlin Alexanderplatz*, in my personal Medina people catalogue bearing the name of Conductor) suggested with careful gestures that we return to the lounge. "I don't speak Czech well enough," he said in his mother tongue, "but you know, we mustn't touch anything." Without a sound, each one sat down at his or her table. Markéta switched off the music. There was nothing to do, except maybe drink. I'd just downed my gin and tonic, when three policemen knocked on the locked glass door.

Medina is the best café in Prague, the Medina waitresses are the nicest girls in this nasty city, Markéta is the nicest of all the Medina waitresses. There was an opinion that Vlasta has no equal, but that could only be thought by people who don't understand the meaning of the Russian phrase "nice girl" that is, basically all the inhabitants of Prague including the local Russian-speakers. Yes, for them —

almost all of them—Vlasta was the queen of Medina, with her doll-like face, light hair, hairstyle à la Marilyn, body of a porn star, deep voice, and a red rose always pinned to her bodice. Paying at the left side of the bar, next to the exhibition of the strangest fruits of the European civilization like "Beer for dogs with taste of meat" or Portuguese mineral water in gorgeous baroque blue glass bottles, all fair trade and ecologically produced, no Moldovan slave was hurt in the production of this drink, I paid a dull compliment to her rose for months, to which she, apparently not seeing through to the dark erotic underside of my heavyweight courteousness, responded with a similarly heavyweight grateful look, casting a glance at her magnificent bust, embellished with the suggestive flower. Saying, *děkuji*. No, I didn't fancy her at all—simply because I didn't fancy her and also, and mostly, because everybody else did. Medina's a special place—here gathers what Russians would call "creative intelligentsia," but thank God, they're no hipsters. Just people the likes of those string players. They fiddle a little and then come here—to drink and have a little gossip. Young expats too. Older folks, like that conductor. I mean of course, I don't know whether he's really a conductor or just some estate manager invited from abroad, but his long manicured fingers, his friendship with the musicians, his similarity to the Fassbinder actor, his silent, peaceful, regular alcoholism—all this makes him a perfect conductor. By the way, this place isn't an alehouse and it's not a bar either. A café in the French style with an Arabic name, placed in a bourgeois district of a Central European capital. They didn't keep sex symbols here, before Vlasta turned up. And now, after her death, they won't either.

But I liked Markéta. I'll be so brave as to say I was a little in love with her, purely platonically or whatever. Her short dark hair, slender figure, the step of a ballerina, gentle, delicate face, decisive voice, all of that was more suitable for Medina than the wild-fantasy corporeality of her colleague. They were real friends, attentive, even affectionate, not only did they not sit idle, delegating orders and glass cleaning to the partner, but quite the contrary; with a cloth and a bottle of detergent held like a gun, one tried to do the work as fast as she could while the other, getting lost in a musical magazine, was having a break with a glass of juice diluted with water. They were a good pair, Vlasta and Markéta. Let me repeat it, I did not come to the café to drool over the waitresses, nobody came here for that, that's what made Medina such a nice place—everybody doing their own thing, some sitting with a glass, some with a book, some in a discussion, and some with a Mac. The background music was entirely suitable, no extremes, with the repertory moving between Coldplay and Nouvelle Vague, quiet, peaceful, cozy dying of the high style, high emotions, high life. European history flowing into the sociology of small communities.

Three policemen knocked on the door, Markéta turned the key in the lock and they entered, first came quite a young one, grim, even grimmer than local inhabitants usually are, maybe he'd been asleep and they woke him up and he had to drive up here, or rather walk, because the police station is around the corner. The second one was old, fat, and kind-looking; about the third there's nothing to say at all, nothing to mention except the traditionally greasy hair, hanging in wisps from under his cap. Regular policemen. They weren't thrilled to be dealing with human issues, lives and especially deaths, but what can you do. Markéta led them to the kitchen. The fat one was back in a minute. He ordered us not to leave the premises without special permission, went outside, locked the door, came back in a couple of minutes with a camera, took it to the kitchen, then picked a vacant table in the lounge and started beckoning us one by one, to do the questioning and write down the testimonies. Markéta offered him tea, and he didn't refuse.

The case was a perfect Agatha Christie. There's only one door to Medina, the entrance door; I know that for certain, as I'd often seen drinks, food, and heavy beer barrels carried to the café. The only way out of the kitchen is through the corridor, which is visible from the lounge. It means there was nobody in the Medina, except myself, the conductor, the string couple, two girls enthusiastically gossiping over a bottle or two of some local stuff all night long, and an old drunk, of the educated sort, who slowly gulped down half a dozen beers every night, watching something on an old-fashioned DVD player. And, of course, Markéta. And Vlasta, but we don't count her—she was killed. That makes it nine people who were in Medina for the past hour to hour and a half, while one of them left for the other world. Well, not actively left, she didn't. Somebody made her leave.

That's the strangest, inexplicable, most terrifying thing about it if, of course, our first thought isn't that the murder itself is something repulsive to the human race. The thing is that being all the time in everybody else's sight, none of us could've slit the poor girl's throat; also, it was impossible to say when exactly it happened. We were all sitting at our tables and doing our things: the conductor was drinking, I was reading my Sebald and sipping through a straw the sweet-and-sour mixture of Gordon's and Kinley, the string players were gulping, talking lazily, smoking and putting out the butts in a green glass ashtray in the sixties' fashion, the girlfriends were chirruping, the old man was watching a film, Markéta . . . What was she doing? She was handing out the drinks. I looked around the tables at which my involuntary accomplices were sitting. It was obvious that during the last two and a half hours it was the conductor who'd ordered drinks (there was still a little whisky in his glass—and he hadn't finished the water), the violin player (half a tankard of Hoegaarden left), and the old man (he was sitting next to me and I saw he poured the rest of his beer into his mouth just before the arrival of the police). And me, of course. I remembered that very well, because I'd come up to the counter to have a chat with Markéta, who was quietly reading an honorably ripped-up book. Since I'd left the position of obituary writer in the local English-language newspaper for the position of Prague consultant for a Berlin gallery, I'd been forced to start pursuing the Czech language seriously. The owner of the gallery was attempting to blow up the European market with the twentieth-century Czech modernism and the role of the dynamite supplier—or rather its inventor—was played by your humble servant. I was paid to roam around the local museums and collections, I had a look at Kupka here, a talk about Diviš there,

I evaluated Šíma's market prospects, heaped dusty trash in antique shops in the search for ancient Czech masterpieces, unknown to the world, and created reports to send to Berlin. Once every two months the gallery owner arrived for a few days, I took her to places where the crème de la crème was waiting, and then was taken by her to an outrageously expensive restaurant where she settled up—with the waiter and with me alike. A dusty job, in the direct sense of the word, but not unpleasant; in any case, it's much better to assist in speculations involving old-fashioned modernism than to speculate about the often non-existent good deeds of the deceased. Amen.

That's why I started to improve my Czech, but how do you learn a language if you don't speak it with your beloved? I didn't follow Byron's rule—my mental resistance to acquiring a Czech girlfriend was apparently stronger than the possible linguistic advantages it could bring; during the past eleven years that I'd spent in Prague I'd gradually turned into a latent recluse, why should I disturb my own solitude anyway, when I can go to Medina and talk to Markéta any evening? Tonight, too, I came up to the bar—to order a second gin and tonic and ask her about the fat volume she was holding in her thin hands. Markéta seemed a little upset and tired, what can a nice young creature be anyway, if she's spent over ten hours supplying tables with alcoholic drinks? On a Friday night, too. "*Crime and Punishment?*" I joked. Markéta looked up at me with her eyes, red with tiredness and thick tobacco smoke, and retorted immediately: "No, no. *Pride and Prejudice.*" She studies literature at university, she has for several years now, I don't understand their system, they're studying, they aren't studying, they're writing final theses, working at the same time, they start a family, go to Britain and Germany to make some money, come back, don't go to classes for months, then they do, then they resume the thesis again. That's what life in Europe is like nowadays, nobody's exerting themselves too much, everybody's living on something, that is, *surviving* on something. But it's some wholly other people, come from the south and the east, who sweep the streets, sit in shops at cash registers, and rebuild old houses for Italian developers. Markéta explained to me that it's time to hand in the thesis, something about protofeminism in nineteenth-century literature, so here she is, tormented by Jane Austen's girls. But I read your Dostoyevsky! The one about the proud beauty who burnt money in the fireplace!

It seems that everybody was busy with their own things, drinking, reading, talking, and nobody, *nobody* went to the kitchen and slit Vlasta's throat. And nobody dropped in to Medina. And it's impossible to sneak through the closed kitchen window, protected by a lattice. Couldn't the girl simply have taken a knife and cut herself? Even if she could, where's the knife? I replayed in my head the film of half an hour ago: the door to the kitchen standing wide open, the microwave with bread lying on it, jars with olives and marinated cheese, the sink, the plates lined up in the cupboards, towels drying on the tap and the back of a chair, the slightly trembling dishwasher. There was no bloody knife, none at all. Certainly not near the dead body of the beauty.

This is what I told the policemen, had a nice little practice in the language, very nice. It needs to be said, they weren't pressing too much, their questions were quite formal, or at least, my own answers surpassed them in details and even interest. But they did nag me, without realizing it themselves. When did you last see the dead woman? I mean, what time? Really, what time? When? I perfectly remember Vlasta behind the bar, in all her power and glory, the Czech Marilyn, smile, a rhinestone necklace on her neck, the red rose, I came in, she nodded to me, then came up to the table and as usual, leant over me as she wrote down the order, showing the color of her bra and emitting a rather strong smell of jasmine. I observed the irregular line of her imperfectly plucked eyebrows, commented on the beautiful summer weather, not too hot, not too cold, just the best time to sit down in a café, and ordered my usual. "Out of lime," she shrugged. Never mind the lime. You don't have a normal Schweppes anyway. Afterwards, she stood at the bar, then walked around the room, wiping the vacant tables. But from what moment wasn't Vlasta seen anymore? When did she go to the kitchen—and more importantly, why? Nobody ordered food at that time, and the people who'd gathered tonight in Medina weren't of the kind who would've cared to propose a toast or get one on their plate.

They kept us for quite some time—first questioning us, then sleepy specialists arrived, went around with brushes and small test tubes, the camera never ceased to work, finally a van stopped at the glass door of Medina, two people with a stretcher got off, solemnly marched past us in the corridor and in a while appeared again, with the stretcher no longer empty. I was sitting, stiff with awe, observing—like in a cop B-movie—the lifeless chubby arm of the victim hanging down, as if the dead girl herself were freeing it from under the sheet that was covering her completely, with only her green converse shoes and the gorgeous light hair to be seen, whose ends, if you looked carefully enough (and I did), were soaked in something brown. The sobered-up gossip-girls cried out, the cellist turned away, Markéta, sitting at my table, was crying. In the door the carriers of the stretcher met with the owner of Medina, who'd been called up in the middle of the night. Petrified, she followed the body with her eyes to the van, didn't move while the stretcher was being pushed in, then the door slammed, the engine sputtered, the tires screeched in the night, and she was still standing there, unable to force herself to enter. And the police didn't rush her.

The following night I called in to Medina, to see Markéta and—won't make a secret out of it—to see how things were going after what had happened the night before, who they'd hired as Vlasta's replacement, whether the music was playing there, which one of the witnesses had returned to the scene of somebody's (*maybe their own*, buzzed in my head) crime. They had found a replacement, the music was playing, the same people were there—only they were sitting at one table, at the head of which, with an even sadder and grimmer look than usual, was sitting the café owner. Markéta nodded to me with an uneasy smile, I responded with a limp wave of my hand and—at the owner's invitation—I sat down at the common table. She wanted to talk to us. They all had the same drink in front of them as almost twenty-four hours before, except the girlfriends, who, considering the obviously mournful tone of the discussion, settled for a glass of wine each. "I'm sure," started the owner of the café, "that you already told the police everything. And the police will find the murderer. Vlasta was ..." Her voice quivered, she sipped some water and continued. "Vlasta was . . . a great girl. Beautiful. Smart. A faultless employee." I found it a little boring, not quite getting why we, knights errant so to speak, should be hearing all this from an almost unknown person about another one, equally unknown. Especially in such an official manner. What can I say about Vlasta? What can I now, twenty hours after her death, remember about her? Her figure, the scent of jasmine, voice, bodice, embellished with the rose ... What else? Oh yes, the hairstyle. The plump throat with the glittering necklace ... Damn, the throat. I shuddered. Dear God, the slit throat. In my mind, I clearly saw that scarlet wound, and the little streams of blood on the white skin, just short of reaching the blood-crimson rose. Something decadent here, frightening obscenity, sick movie, Rosemary's baby ... The puzzled novice waiter glanced out from the corridor and called to Markéta, who was standing at our table, with a cloth in one hand, and a spray bottle for cleaning the tables in the other. "Where are the knives and forks?" he whispered loudly. "What?" "Knives and forks." "In the drawers, I told you." "There's too few, it's not enough." "Impossible." "True. Not enough." "Search wherever you want. Everything's in the drawers." I'd never seen her be so mean, I had never even imagined her like that, but what would I be like in her place, with a cloth in my hand, with the same people as last night, when she found the body of her friend in the kitchen, soaked in blood, with the same people, one of whom may be the heartless murderer. A telephone rang, Markéta fell on to her backpack that was standing by the bar, clumsily pulled the zipper and the contents fell out onto the wooden floor of Medina: a notebook, pen, cigarettes, wallet, some receipts, crumpled paper tissues, compact powder ... A corner of the huge Austen volume was peeking out carefully from the open backpack jaw, as if not trusting the invitation to take a walk in the smoke-filled air and down a glass or two in the company of the nicest and smartest young people in Prague. The conductor bent down and handed to Markéta the lighter that had landed next to his long legs. Then the old man buried himself under the table, dug there a long time and finally pulled out a small elegant piece, which I, surprised, recognized as a USB stick, sprinkled with rhinestones. I had seen the likes of it in Swarovski shops. Cool. Bravo, Markéta.

Embarrassed, she threw the things back into the backpack, answered the phone, and went to the neighboring table to spray and wipe, spray and wipe. She's really awfully nice, it wouldn't be bad ... what wouldn't be bad?! I didn't finish the indecent thought, when Markéta yelled somewhere to the side: "Hey! Hey! Honza! Just remembered! It's all in the dishwasher!" and ran to the kitchen. Ah Honza, you lucky boy. I started thinking about how, let's say, a person's dying, or even being murdered, like Vlasta, now she is and in a moment is no longer, and things carry on undisturbed, not paying any attention to what's happening, the bread was lying on the microwave *before*, and so it's lying *now*, some ham was lying in the fridge, and so it continues to lie now without any remorse, see, even the dishwasher hasn't been emptied yet, and maybe it was Vlasta herself who switched it on ... Things treat us, the warm-blooded, with indifference, verging on contempt. We live, suffer, rejoice, die, but they last until the time when they most serenely stop lasting, unemotionally as usual. We're surrounded by a cold world that doesn't give a shit, it's not us who are the masters of things, but they're ours, and our slavery is deeper and stranger than what we usually take for the meaning of the word. We aren't in control of things; they impassively observe us, like a CCTV. I imagined how the dishwasher undisturbedly fulfilled its usual duty at the same moment, when. Did the murderer hear its rustle? In any case, water pouring in its bowels and the whirr of the engine were the last sounds that ever reached the ears of the dying waitress.

In fact, any one of us could've done it, I thought. And none of us too. This is life and not the cinema, and not Agatha Christie. No motives for you, no aunt's inheritance, no jealousy, no revenge. The whole thing isn't hot or cold, just cool, cool in the European way, half-accidental people in a lovely café with nice waitresses, one of whom . . . Really, every one of the patrons—including myself, by the way—could've picked the right moment when Vlasta left for the kitchen, then got up in no hurry, walked away as if in the direction of the bathroom, stepped through the open door, come up from behind and slit her throat. A matter of a second. Nothing special, a bloody quickie. And then you'd better get away quick yourself, hiding the knife before you do. But now it's getting mysterious. Where do you hide the thing, dripping with blood? The policemen searched us too, and didn't find anything suitable in the whole establishment. And also, the girl wouldn't stand with her back to the visitor who'd walked into the kitchen. And one last thing. Anybody could've done it, no doubt, but would have to do it swiftly, otherwise what if somebody hears something and comes in. I looked at the people sitting at the table. An old withered drunkard. Giggling gossips. Certainly not them. And the rest? It's virtually impossible to walk past the bar, and past Markéta, hoping she won't notice. This is some Chesterton. Fishermen's club, of course. And then, well all right, let it be that way, but there's a question—what was she doing in the kitchen?

Medina closed early, I stayed till the venetian blinds were lowered, Markéta switched off the lights, let Honza go first, then me, locked the door, put the key into her backpack, her colleague, shouting something on the way, hurried after the bus that was slowing down, and we were left alone. You know everything, she said. No, not everything. What don't you? You guess. All right, later. We came to a high slope over the central station, drowned in the heavy scents of trees too southern for this region, silently walked above the chains of parallel blue lights that converged and diverged in the darkness, on the left they disappeared into even thicker darkness in which you could intuit the entrance into an underground tunnel, on the right they crept up to large platforms, lit by dim bluish light, with arches, also emitting dim light. Behind it all spread the lively fires of the city at night: yellow, white, and red; from the general darkness only the bodies of churches and temples stood out, lit from underneath, with lights of the landing planes twinkling above. During such an evening nothing matters at all, nothing has any meaning, you can do and say anything. I'd given up smoking years before, but now I'd give half my life for the sweetish first puff. So how did you know? The dishwasher. Dishwasher? Yes. You put the knife into the dishwasher and turned it on. It was still working when you shouted for us to hear. A faint smile. I was proud that I'd thought of it. Very fine. Witty, too. Evidence destroyed before our eyes, blood and fingerprints washed off the knife for half an hour, in everybody's presence, and we, simpletons, wouldn't realize. And we didn't! Well yes. But there's something else. What? Only you alone could have asked her to tidy the kitchen before closing time. Nobody was ordering any food. Yes, a mistake. Another faint smile. I was waiting for the girlfriends to get peckish. Two bottles of white wine, a couple of joints, I saw them smoking outside, and nothing. I waited and waited, was furious, but had to do it. Couldn't wait till tomorrow. Why? No, a different question: what did you need her USB stick for? Money. What money? It costs no more than three thousand. No, my money. Yours? Well yes, she was trying to get money from me. How so? I'm a Catholic. And? And I have a boyfriend. I live with my parents. Couldn't bring him home. So? I stayed the nights in Medina and he fucked me. Lovely idea! Well yes. But that bitch saw us and recorded it on her phone. I mean, on her phone and her Macbook camera too. She's studying at a film school. *Was* studying. A faint smile. Yes, was studying. So. She left her Mac open in the kitchen, started something for the time needed, hid herself with her phone. Just imagine, we're there doing God knows what, she jumps out, says, darlings, I caught you red-handed. We had a laugh over it, decided it was a joke, had a drink together and forgot about it. But she made a video clip from the footage, saying, pay me or I'll upload it to Pornplay. I thought again she was joking but she showed me the video, copied it to the glittering USB stick before my eyes, deleted it from everywhere else and solemnly announced that the thing is for sale for ten thousand crowns, the bitch. To be paid within three days. The stick will be hanging on my neck, so that you remember. What could I do? And you killed your friend for six hundred dollars? I don't have the money. She said, your parents are rich, take it from them. But they don't have it either. Too bad for her now. Underneath, a belated train went by, empty, lit by dead grayish light, stopping at the platform it sputtered, waited for a few moments, turned off the lights and silently set out for the sidetrack, heading somewhere behind the station. A police car slowly passed us, from its open window we heard an announcer's quiet voice telling us the news of the restless world. We came to the recently built bourgeois houses, iron, glass, huge TV screens emitting bluish waves into the half-empty rooms, furnished with all the taste of the middle-class magazines, and we turned back. Grim teenagers were dissolving from the park on the hill. We stopped at the corner of my street. All right, here I am. Good. This here — she dug in her backpack, got something out, and put it in my hand — take it. It'd be a pity to throw it out and I don't need it.

Once at home, I didn't even take off my coat, I sat down at the computer straight away and opened the file from the drive. A half of a boy is performing feverish moves, as if trying to trample something in the lower part of the girl's body that's on all fours, her knees on a chair, her hands pushing against the worktop of the cupboard. The resolution is quite high, on the left half of the girl's butt we can see a tattoo in the form of a dove, circled by a motto. The words aren't clear enough to read. The boy is thin, with almost no hair. Then dimmer scenes follow, shot from another angle. They show the same couple doing the same things, but the viewer has a somewhat different perspective, we can see the girl's fringe, covering her eyes, the curve of her neck, a little cross hanging from it. The partner is almost unseen, except the fatless belly towering over her backside and a part of his chest. His hands are on the girl's hips, the resolution doesn't allow us to see whether his fingers dig into her flesh or not. The whole video lasts two minutes and forty-one seconds, it's silent, it's skillfully edited and leaves a great aesthetic impression. No, it leaves a great emotional impression. No, it leaves you seeing red and your chest bursting. No, simply — you can't stop watching it. It's the perfect work of art that doesn't have any relation to life. This is much more than life, this is hardcore. Vlasta, jasmine beauty with a rose at your breast, your death was not in vain.

An Other Plot

To A. L.

It's been a long time since I stopped watching local TV. Since they forced all the inhabitants of the Bohemian-Moravian Palatinate of the European Union to buy mysterious little boxes in order to receive fifteen local channels instead of four. I bought one too. I brought it home, connected it to the television set and discovered that there's only so much I can watch — either the local programming or three hundred channels in various languages, which were hidden in my old little box, connected to the antenna. But by that time, something funny was happening with that box too. The channels were disappearing one after another, and especially those that I used to watch, rare as that was. A pure mockery: the idiotic CNN and the Russian RT are where they should be, no worries, but for instance Arte is gone. It was namely the loss of Arte that finished me off — it was there that long documentaries about the lives of Mongolian nomads or Brazilian Indians used to be on, and once I even got to watch the film adaptation of *The Magic Mountain* there — didn't understand one word in German but I know the novel almost by heart! The look of Steiger, playing Peeperkorn, is enough to make you cry.

First the desertion of Arte and the German pop-channel where they still played refreshing Teutonic music videos, then the arrival of the strange little box with fifteen highly unnecessary Czech channels — these are the reasons why I, never a TV addict anyway, stopped pursuing this activity completely. Only at times, after I've spent all evening in Medina, or come back home after the usual report on the situation of the market in Czech modernism of the twenties and thirties, I switch on the box where they speak all possible languages except the local one, find a Saudi channel, turn off the sound and play the first CD I can find from the gift edition of *The Ring of the Nibelung*. West meets East, the Teutonic with the Arabian, the last Hajj of the Valkyries. Nice background music for a nap before going to bed.

On the whole, I don't watch TV. And I don't browse the local websites (except the gallery, museum, and antique ones). I read newspapers only 1) in the line for the doctor, notary public, or barber, or 2) aboard Czech Airlines, where they're handed out at the entrance. As we know, all electronic devices, fuck them, have to be switched off during takeoff and landing—it's therefore in these moments, having drawn a curtain over the screen of my beloved iPad, that I start examining the Czech press. Here's our *Lidové noviny*[14] and *Dnes*,[15] and something else too. That's how it was this time. In the hideous Sheremetyevo airport, where they tortured us in a hundred different ways, where in order to reach your seat by the window of the fat iron bird, you've got to show your passport six times (I counted!), where in the dark little chamber, people with greenish faces throw a plastic tray under your feet, take off your shoes, show us your boring socks, take off your belt, hands up, don't keep your pants from falling down, and then the long gloomy corridors of the terminal, built by the old, previous authorities, those who'd attached so many meanings to the technical term "currency," each one worse than the next. Now the currency meanings have crept down the gray Sheremetyevo corridors, and sparkle in the glasses of the watches, exhibited next to the duty-free bottles, nice that they let you use the Wi-Fi free of charge but there's only one thing you want, to run into the plane as soon as possible, stick your coat, bereft of all heat by now, into the overhead compartment, cast a look through the window at the lights shimmering on the runway, and open a Czech newspaper.

And there's a photo on the fifth page: an empty flight of steps, copying the tilt of a slope, leading down from the large buildings from the end of the nineteenth century, with tennis courts on its right and left, and a handrail welded from iron pipes next to it. A sitting man is leaning against one of the posts, wearing a light-colored coat, funny clown-like shoes with long sharp tips, even slightly twisted upwards, with his head hanging down to his chest. Strange. There aren't many drunkards in this city, that is, there aren't many in the streets—of course I don't mean in the alehouses or at

14 People's News
15 Today

home—but outside are only German tourists, and those don't go
to this part of the city. I recognized the flight of steps, it leads to Albertov, away from the faculties of physics and medicine, it's empty,
the steps are at places lined with some bushes, overgrown and very
Russian-looking, the likes of which you can find in a forsaken part
of a park in some ex-proletarian former-Soviet city, but these here
are watched from above by the European Science, Positivism, that is
conveyed to us through the presence of the huge peeling buildings
from the era of overwhelming eclecticism.

He was sitting, with his head dropped down onto his chest, but
if you looked at the photo before you saw the headline "RUSSIAN
DEATH IN ALBERTOV," you could see a white stripe, something
like a narrow scarf connecting the handrail to the man's neck, which
was drowned between the big head and the fat chest—the stripe
was fastened to the place where the handrail created a T with the
vertical post against which the body was leaning. In another newspaper the same photo bore the headline "DEATH BY THE PO-
LICE MUSEUM."

The museum is indeed nearby, just a little further, if you don't
turn right toward the steps, but walk along the street leading from
the lunatic asylum with a shady half-neglected park, fenced off by
a tall stone wall, a Jesuit baroque church stands above, badminton
is played on the park's trampled courts if the season's right. Starting at the lunatic asylum, the street continues, past the museum of
Dvořák, a few hospitals built in various styles, ranging from the factory style of the nineteenth-century red brick to the glass and gray
concrete of the last third of the twentieth century, then the university buildings begin, and here, if you don't dive in between two huge
temples of science but take a straight route, you'll find yourself next
to a small, round Gothic church standing above a large ravine, with
a frightening bridge leading from it, renowned for jumping sui-
cides; below lies the Nusle district of the city, an area which used to
be full of gardens; Kafka would plant his beet in one of them. And
from there on follow houses, streets, the railway, the life, but the
little park right next to the church is empty, only a wretched poster

is fluttering in the wind with the name of the regular exhibition in the Police Museum that's for some reason located here. I usually didn't come this far on my lonely walks, but turned, went down between the tennis courts, then passed the experimental gardens of the university botanists; on the right side, almost just before the descent, there's another faculty building, another resemblance to some ex-Soviet place and its medicine academy buildings; this is where the nostalgic part ends and one starts that's wholly different—the decrepit and magnificent back of beyond of the Austro-Hungarian Empire. Emptiness. Indeed, it's always empty here. Then you pass a few big dirty houses on the way to the river bank, it's a meeting point for people when the weather's good, on the weekends there's a market here with those kind of things that would be called "bio" in countries west of the Czech Republic. Since I started visiting these parts on business, I don't feel comfortable walking around here anymore, like I'm committing an incest of business and leisure; it's been half a year since I last went to Albertov on the weekend. But on working days I come to see a former compatriot here, as wealthy a one as they come, as nervous a miser as they come, and an art collector, as they sometimes come. I've got to tell him about Váchal and Kupka, refuse his whisky and vodka, pass over his little jokes in silence, and tear my eyes away from the bric-a-brac that has filled up his decent-sized apartment. The last one isn't that difficult: I focus on my iPad, thank you, my electronic friend, pretending that I'm reminding myself of names of the works and creative periods. There's nothing you can do, Mr. Vladimir Ivanovich has decided to fork out, so I've got to suffer. I suffered as recently as two days ago, after which I flew to Moscow.

The plane took off, I stuck the unfinished newspaper into the seat pocket and buried myself in a book randomly picked out of the gadget depths. It wasn't until the plane started to descend before landing that I returned to the strange man who'd decided to die at the Albertov flight of steps. Why would it be a "Russian" death? Did they guess by the pathetic shoes? But even the locals wear those kind of shoes nowadays and about five years ago the Italians started to wear them too, although not exactly those Italians who ride here on buses to have a good time, holding hands like children, in padded jackets, swearing at each other in guttural voices, freezing and going crazy from the extent of the stupid baroque. I could never understand their need to leave the good baroque and go to see the bad one. What kind of downshifting is this? The newspaper that mentioned the Russian part of the incident said that his phone was in the Cyrillic alphabet, and so were the cards in his purse, so that's how they knew where he was from. "The police are trying to identify the victim and discover the cause of death." Well yes. Here's a Russian walking unhurriedly around the hospitals and instead of reaching the Police Museum and the suicidal bridge, he ties himself to the handrail and dies. Alone, so to speak. From grief and homesickness.

At home it all looked rather neglected; playing ducks and drakes together with a little distracted life of the past month had brought my headquarters to a state of slight disarray, and I decided to do it in style and get the cleaning lady. While I'm going about my business, she can impose order upon the modest dwelling of a man without means. Her name is Sofia, I've known her for eight years or more, she's a quiet, intimidated woman from Perm with a rich past and a poor, almost destitute present. That's what happens. In the mid-nineties, when the visa wasn't yet a necessity, when the former Soviet peoples were heading for the freshly sliced-off Czech Republic, Sofia sold her large apartment and decided to start living the peaceful life of a guesthouse-owner. She viewed a house in Marienbad, then bought it, then it became clear that the person who sold it to her wasn't the owner. Left with no house and no money, the former Perm art historian who specialized in traditional wooden sculpture became a cleaning lady and a live-out nanny. I met Sofia at a time when she'd already left the state of horrible poverty, having moved to the level of normal, local poverty, at which any amount of stuff you buy in the supermarket costs up to a hundred crowns, no more. She wasn't the best cleaner but she was a caring one, she lovingly dusted my books, even asked me if she could borrow some to read; I confess, I had a suspicion that Sofia was drinking—her hands were shaking, and an eloquent flush shone on her cheeks, but then I realized that it's stress, anxiety, and most likely the first stage of diabetes. My mother had looked similar, also working as a cleaning lady at the beginning of the nineties, and diabetes tortured her to death within seven years. Her hands were shaking too; the similarity was added to by the fact that the hands of both one and the other were oddly strong, very strong: I remember from my childhood the burning pain when my mother hit me with a wet cloth; as for the cleaning lady, she could open the lid of any jar of jam, no matter how obstinate it was.

Enough gossip now: I asked her to come the morning after my arrival. At ten fifteen, having prolonged the mummification of my body, I bumped into her in the doorway. Sofia was visibly not her usual self, it was obvious something had happened to her, she was bashful about it but some weighty trouble, some malignant tumor was swelling her from within, pressing on her; she was collecting the cloths and sponges with insecure hands, dropped a bottle of detergent, I was checking my pockets in silence, making sure I'd taken everything, finally couldn't restrain myself any longer and asked what had happened, anything wrong with her health? I'm in trouble. What is it, if I may ask? Do you need help? My courtesy is indifferent, neither hot nor cold, and I'm sure to get spit out of we-know-whose mouth, but although indifferent, I was honestly imitating worries. So, do you need help? How could you help me . . . Got the summons from the police. Something wrong with the papers? Visa? Indeed, what kind of problems can a Russian have, living here—only those that are caused by the ownership of that goddamn red book, the passport, which is the source of eternal, humiliating, Kafkaesque trouble. The evil empire—or, the former evil empire, currently no empire at all—stands and falls not on the ancient three whales but on one stinky hippopotamus, a bucket-headed leviathan, whose name is "humiliation"; for the inhabitants of that crumb of territory, serfdom is issued in the form of those little books that you're obliged to show everywhere and at all times, like the yellow ticket, like a shameful report from the venereal clinic,

like torn nostrils and a purple brand on the shoulder; having abandoned the former evil E., you become a slave not of the country but
of the little book; you shall not lose it or keep it secret; you shall not
show it without additional little stickers, and it's all sorts of trouble
to even hand it back, like a Karamazov ticket. This is how you run
between the representatives of the country that was and the guard-
ians of the purity of the one that is now. So what—I asked Sofia—
is it about the visa? No, it's a questioning. I used to clean the place of
one of our people, and he got killed. Killed? Killed. Or simply died.
I don't know. They're questioning everybody, so they asked me to
come too. Why are you worried, Sofia? It wasn't you who . . . er . . .
killed him. But you know them, they don't care, they're all ready to
sweep it under the carpet, especially if it's a Russian. And my Czech's
bad. Don't worry, they'll give you a translator. They have to. It's in
their own interest. Don't worry. All's going to be well. Don't take it
too hard. But if you do need some help . . . she nodded, I nodded in
response and carefully closed the door behind me.

I was having coffee in Ebel when the police called me. At first
I took the officer for one of those modern salespeople (may they
rot!), who try to force on you an unnecessary contract for another
telephone number or an even more unnecessary mortgage. Thus
I spoke in a stern voice and with a merciless intonation. What do
you want? The poor girl had to repeat it for a second and third time
before I realized that I had to take to my heels, documents in my
pockets, and hasten to the such and such department in such and
such street. Concerning what, was all I was able to say, licking my
coffeed lips, what happened? We are investigating the circumstances
of the death of Mr. Okurov. Sorry, who? Mr. Okurov. We found
your number in his telephone. Are you speaking now from your
own phone? Yes. So, we're expecting you. Yes. Do you need us to
send the summons? No, I don't. There were a few local newspapers
in the café, which I usually don't read there (see above), preferring
a lazy observation of life or a book. I took from a hook in the wall
a wooden frame with a tattered copy of the *Noviny* and started to
read with a feeling of detestation. Aha, here it is. Albertov. The flight

of steps. The man tied to it. Russian. Identified. Okurov. *Vladimír Ivanovič*, as they spelled it. But he's supposed to be buying three works of Diviš on Friday!

The shaking of my hands added some drama to the following scene: I touched the wrong keys several times, when looking up Sofia's number. She was already walking outside, it means my home's clean and tidy, I thought mechanically, but the knowledge, usually so pleasant, it's nice to crawl to a clean apartment in the evening, with a faint scent of detergents, to stand a little in the hall, brooding lazily, maybe I should start cleaning myself, for financial reasons and to maintain my inner discipline, so to speak, care for oneself and so on, but not now, I had to promptly, right now, without leaving the high pouffe by the wooden bar counter, over which was hanging an ancient map of Africa, hear that things are not how I think they are, that it's just a coincidence, a silly, ridiculous coincidence, that her employer wasn't called Okurov at all, not Vladimir Ivanovich at all, yes, again, hello Sofia, I've got a wholly irrelevant question, sorry, what was it? and do you happen to know the last name too? where? Ke Karlovu?

The street where Vladimir Ivanovich Okurov lived was called Ke Karlovu, his house stands opposite that park where I used to play badminton next to the lunatic asylum. Well-known places, they say. Somewhere around those places the idiot Švejk used to live, but I find it doubtful, taking into account how the soldier moved about, especially in that wheelchair under the control of Mrs. Müller. In any case, Švejk came here to drink. That's a fact. And I, at some point, started coming here to make money, I mean coming in the hope of making it, but never mind, it did pay a little. My new client dwelled on the second floor of a reconstructed, re-built house; didn't even dwell, but stayed at times, always on a few weeks' stop on the way between Riga and Barcelona. As the Okurov family had settled down in Catalonia, his business was probably in the capital of the Governorate of Livonia. What he was dealing with in Prague, I don't know, but he did furnish his apartment in a solid way. And at some point he felt a great need for local art to add to all the Indian furniture, plasma-screen televisions, and Meissen porcelain. So that's how I got there. The landlord received me sitting in an armchair, with a damaged leg cast in plaster, a wrapped wrist, and a scratched face, excuse the look, I've been skiing in Harrachov. I made an awkward joke about sport being detrimental to man's health, and we sat down to business.

Vladimir Ivanovich had an overwhelming enthusiasm. Locked in plaster armor, Okurov traveled around galleries and antique shops in his wheelchair—and that with the absence of any special elevators, or ramps, or anything of the like except in his own house. But he quickly started walking on crutches, and then on his own legs. I can't say he had awful taste; on the contrary, he knew quite a lot, quietly understood things, had a modest sense of art, the sense of both the connoisseur and the trader. But when, a few months later, Okurov had the idea to hang and exhibit the booty in his apartment, I froze. I didn't know where to look. I opened my iPad and lied that I had to promptly respond to an email. Taken together, his purchases created a strange landscape, not of the Czech painting and sculpture of the previous century, not of some particular period or style, but . . . the Devil knows what. To put it in the old-fashioned way, it was a landscape of his soul, if that exists at all. Or, if we want to express it in other words, the structure of his consciousness, built upon the chaos of the unconscious. Something like that. Eighteen works of art—ranging from surrealism to postmodernism, from figurative to abstract, from Toyen to Skála—that, put together, created a sense of unbearable ugliness, emitted the stink of a monstrous mix of cowardice, greed, cruelty, and cheap pathos—a mixture that had nothing in common with any single one of those works. I was devastated by the result, deafened by the thought that, by selecting these things, I had taken part in a crime against humanity; I was crushed by guilt, penitence, and disgust. Context, smacking, was gorging on the phenomena, and it was me who'd thrown coal into its infernal furnace. Thank God, Okurov disappeared to Barcelona rather quickly, and I returned to other business, not as profitable, but certainly not as sinister.

From that time on he didn't break his legs, so he came here only rarely, staying in Prague for three or four days, no longer. I always found something interesting for him, he bought it or didn't, adding new exhibits to his demonic collection; however, their overall number almost didn't change—Vladimir Ivanovich was able to find buyers for the Czech art in France and was selling them some pieces, with quite a profit for himself, it has to be noted. This man had a nose, he definitely did. This time I'd reserved some of Diviš's graphics for his arrival, reckoning that the prison darkness of that hapless fellow would overcome the general spirit of the Okurov collection. But it won't now, ever.

I went to the police station, in my mind going through the little that I knew about Vladimir Ivanovich. That is, almost nothing. Where he was originally from and how he came to be in Prague, Barcelona, or Riga, I had no idea. Not even the faintest. Okurov had a Uralian accent, and that's it, as far as his genealogy goes. He had a photo standing on the table, a lady of about fifty and a sweet-looking girl. They were most likely the inhabitants of Catalonia. No traces of other people or of any previous life were seen in Vladimir Ivanovich's apartment, everything was bought here in Prague, no personal history, only current stories unfolding here, based on the fact that a lot of things of various origin found themselves next to each other, from the now unnecessary wheelchair on the balcony to the vanishing lines of Šimotová's draft on the wall. All that—wholly unpoetically, of course, and taking into account my clumsy Czech, I told the tired investigator. He had a young policewoman sitting behind him; the pattering of her manicured fingers fully reflected the rhythm of my concise narration. They, of course, were interested in his money—and in the answer to a funny little question, which they didn't ask me directly, whether it was me who killed Mr. Okurov. I didn't even burst out laughing. No, not me. No, I didn't have to. Yes, we were getting ready for another purchase. No, he didn't give me an advance. No, I don't know where he kept it. The collection of Vladimir Ivanovich wasn't touched; from the apartment, if we're to believe the live-out cleaning lady, nothing disappeared, except the landlord himself of course, who was by some unknown means transferred to the Albertov steps, where he was found choked, tied to a post, dressed in a gray coat. Those places are empty, there are no CCTV cameras, the few passersby didn't see either a fight or Okurov himself, in case it was he who had a wish to walk down the flight of steps, put a cord around his neck, tie its end to the handrail, sit down comfortably, and strangle himself. At this point we said goodbye, after the unavoidable signature under the unclearly print-ed testimony record that crawled out of the old-fashioned machine.

They didn't find the murderer, if there'd been one at all. I don't think they were searching too hard anyway. I wouldn't be worrying about it myself—due to my antipathy towards the deceased and to my mental laziness too. He died, so he died, it's no reason for any particular worries. A month had passed, full of some unimport-ant stuff, an exhibition, a couple of sales, an article for a Moscow magazine, disclosing the Czech art's newly discovered beauty to the Russian rich; here I was again, coming back from the regular travel home, and again I decided to have a feast of laziness and hedonism. Sofia agreed to come in two days, which didn't exactly suit me, as I was planning to work at home but what can you do, you declared yourself a Rockefeller, so get the hell out of the apartment, so that you aren't getting in the cleaning lady's way. I hadn't seen her since that time and I almost didn't recognize her at first. She was a differ-ent person—tranquil, self-assured, her hands didn't tremble any-more, the frightened look alone was giving away the former victim of the post-Soviet period. I couldn't help it and gave her a com-pliment. Thank you, she said. I've been on a holiday. Damn this shit, what's going on here, how could *she* go on a holiday? Where? What for? Not noticing my bewilderment, Sofia started to take out of the storage room the bottles with detergents for the floor and furniture. Where, if I may ask, did you go? I went home, to Perm. She hadn't been there for about ten years, I knew that for certain, she had nobody left there. Her husband died in the mid-nineties, far as I understood, right after the death of their daughter, Lisa, to whom, as I was told by that acquaintance who'd introduced me to

Sofia, some kind of tragedy happened. Either she died, or there was something else too, I can't remember exactly. If not a huge darkness, then at least a cloud. And how are things there? Actually, pretty well. They've cleaned up the city, built a lot of new things, there are big red letters in the streets, a new museum has been opened. Well yes, Gelman. But how does she . . . ? Oh, I forgot completely, art historian, the Komi sculpture. She knows museums, she's got to.

In the café, where I went to kill time, they had such fast Wi-Fi that I started to wander around the Net distractedly — instead of working, of course. I really didn't feel like drudging now. I leafed through the newspaper apps. Scrolled down the Twitter posts. Burrowed in Facebook. Looked at the pictures from the Lucian Freud exhibition in London, hmmm, would love to go there. It was still too early to return home, and too late to start working on the unfinished text now; I remembered Perm and typed in the search engine box "museum perm rubakhina." Nothing. Well yes, she left there before the appearance of any Russian internet. Or at any rate, before the appearance of any Russian internet in the Russian province. All right then. What else can we look up? Aha, Freud, what are the critics writing. My attention was distracted by a woman of exquisite beauty, she looked into the lounge but left immediately, as if pulled outside by an unknown force. I saw through the window that she was being pulled by the hand by a little boy, fat, content, and dull. Children. Awful. The woman wasn't paying any special attention to him until he finally, from pure stupidity, stamped in a puddle of water, decorating himself, her legs, and the trousers of a passing clerk, with brown spatters of mud. She gave him such a slap that the kid didn't even start crying immediately; he was standing there staring at her in surprise, as if not getting how's that and what's happening, where is this coming from but suddenly his face twisted, softened, reddened — and if it hadn't been for the merciful window glass, all of us, the patrons of the Black Rose, would've gone deaf from the piercing cry. I dropped my eyes to the screen and what nonsense: instead of the reviews about the exhibition of the great artist, I saw a list of links to some Lucan. I even managed a thought about how cool this is, the culture's blooming, there's so much written on the internet about the forgotten author of the *Pharsalia*, but alas, it was all different, the topic there was some popular story, this fellow, Lord Lucan, disappeared a quarter of a century ago, all covered in blood, he killed the nanny, he beat the wife, didn't touch the children, he vanished, sightings are reported from Kenya, Niger, South Africa, America, God knows where, the police are searching, the army are searching, the public are searching, stupid shit, I just typed Lucan instead of Lucian. The comic and the cosmic. A difference of one sibilant.

I can't sit at the table any more, I'll go and have a walk, I've got half an hour left. I went out and wandered along the quietly rustling London Street, lined by trees, which is a rare thing in these parts, green's coming out on the branches, another couple of days and everything here will be blossoming, naïvely celebrating, like the *Ode to Joy*, only who else except me ever notices, very few people walk along this street. A few servants of the Temple of Aesthetic Surgery that has settled in the former offices of a telephone company run across it, a few young ladies from the nearby school of economics walk past, otherwise it's all my territory, I alone walk here, and take for my own in my free time this city space free from any meaning. I turned right at the restaurant that's in the place of the former Art 'n' Choke, in times past it felt so nice to cool my badminton sweat there with a tankard of Pilsner or a glass of white wine with stuffed olives, where has the time gone, nowadays there's something needless here, never mind, what badminton, what Pilsner, I crossed Belgrade Street, walked down a short street where an awful emptiness always reigns, just like in the Petersburg district of Kolomna, there's a tunnel under the railway, a small isle between one pair of rails and the other, two hotels face each other, then another underground passageway, and I turned round a hospital on the left, and walked past another hospital, built of red bricks. I left the Okurov house behind me. I haven't been to these places since that time.

A funny thing to see—a parking lot for wheelchairs in the hospital yard, something between a parking lot in front of a supermarket and the place where you leave its shopping trolleys. How do they find those they need? Hardly by inventory numbers, it's unlikely that anybody would take the pains to sort them in rows and put them in nice order, and they're different too—some are old, many times painted in strong colors, and some are the nickeled ones, they almost look elegant, not too many of those, but there are a few. I wonder, do they ever change their construction. For instance, if we compared the one in which Müller used to drive about the brave idiot, and the one that's standing right next to the fence. I made use of the quite wide opening and crawled in, so that I could touch the cold metal of the construction. How is it that they don't get stolen? Who'd need them anyway? But no, you can always bring and sell it to the scrapyard—that means they get stolen. Or not. A nurse passed by, not turning her head to me, without a single word she took one of the wheelchairs and drove it to the side of the hospital building; I made my way to the street and met her again, she was moving a sturdy man to the hospital opposite, well what a job, the man's sitting with a pale face void of all interest, he's wearing a coat, thrown over his hospital pajamas, staring into the sky, a passerby had to get out of their way, the pavement is narrow, the wretched guy stepped right into a puddle. I walked up to the Police Museum. Enjoying the view of Nusle and Vyšehrad, I turned back, came up to the beginning of the flight of steps leading downwards, the branches here were still naked, it seems these bushes bloom later, it's here that poor Okurov was sitting, although why poor, I'd very much like to know how much the Catalonian next of kin got, who's living now in the nearby apartment, and where the pictures I'd collected ended up. On the way back I played the role of the wretched passerby—a perfectly dried-up nurse sped up her hospital carriage so much that the passenger sitting on it yelled out to me to get out of the way! Clear the road! So I had the honor of meeting the hospital puddle too.

She hadn't gone yet. Lining up the chairs, she was returning the things to the state of order which I'd set once and for all times, the order without which they were losing their meaning or, even worse, were acquiring a wholly different one, inimical, nasty, aggressive.

Chopsticks are supposed to lie perpendicular, people to conform
to some social classification, sounds to the rhythm of the cosmic
metronome, causes unavoidably bear their consequences, otherwise
we get a suicidal chaos and a shoe smeared with dirt. Sofia felt my
paranoia regarding the only possible order of things and conscientiously ordered them after the inevitable moving during the cleaning. I knew about it but this was the first time that I found her
doing it. I settled down in the kitchen, so as not to get in her way
and again opened the curtain of the iPad. In the two windows Safari was hunting two different prey. In the first was the mysterious
villain Lord Lucan, having taken the place of Freud's great-nephew
in the Google search box, in a moment of madness he was killing
the nanny with a lead pipe, threatening his wife, hiding himself
at the place of some fellow aristocrats, disappearing in Africa, appearing in Africa, those who have seen him please let us know in
such and such message box. There's now a live 24/7 LORD LUCAN
MESSAGE BOARD to report sightings and express your views and
news. The other window was empty, the search engine was ignoring
"museum perm rubakhina," I started to delete the request left to
right and when the first word disappeared from the box, leaving the
other two, a list rolled out immediately underneath on the screen,
a bunch of links provided with Dostoyevskian opening lines about
the hapless girl, about the search for the runaway rich man, about
the spoiled children and the social abyss. What on earth was happening in Perm fifteen years ago?

It'd been two hours since Sofia went away and I was still sitting
in the kitchen and musing. Strange, but all this heap of facts, symbols, insignificant details, untrue images, and nervous premonitions
that had been wrapping up around me for the past month, it didn't
create a logical chain before, each link of which would be cast of
highly resistant alloy, its form economical and perfect, one thing
flowing into another. I ran through the story once again, which had
opened in the other window. Well yes, a lord, whether a drunkard
or a drug addict or a maniac, whether he beat the poor nanny to
death, or, as he was saying himself, just saw through the window

how somebody was doing it, but nobody believes Lucan, because he ran away from the crime scene, hid for a few days at his friends', and then disappeared. He was allegedly seen a few years later, then he was allegedly seen again, in another place, you can have a look at the photo, an uninteresting guy with a moustache, a movie villain, the BBC writes that somebody recognized him, maybe he's still alive, sitting in some middle of nowhere, calmly sipping cocktails, collecting Japanese erotic engravings or whatever people collect. And in the other Safari window we have the rough Perm of the mid-nineties, nouveau riche in a comical red (certainly) jacket, with the manners of a social upstart, they got a student from a poor family to look after the daughter, she didn't look carefully enough, the little girl wrapped a swing cord around her neck, all in all, they noticed it in time, saved the girl, punished the nanny, threw her into a cold cellar for three days, half-naked, with her hands tied behind her back; when they came downstairs again, they found she'd hanged herself, she managed to untie the knot and choked herself from the fear and humiliation. The nouveau riche ran away. The family disappeared. Allegedly, they've been seen in Spain. The nanny was from an educated family.

Well whatever, like country, like Lucans. I'm indifferent to morality but I'm strongly interested in the structure and succession of events. Let's say, she was already here, in the Czech Republic, when all that happened. She never saw the nouveau riche. He'd clearly changed his surname. She was cleaning in his apartment and accidentally came across something. Put two and two together. Uralian accent, nothing more. Aha, that's him, for sure. She had nothing to lose—after the death of her daughter and husband. What then? That is, not what. *How?*

Of course, the strong hands. For example, he was sitting on the sofa, or on a chair in the kitchen. She was bustling around with brooms. Came up from behind and quickly choked him, a matter of a second, I remember how she could deal with the jar lids. And then the complicated part starts—to get the wheelchair from the balcony, drag the body onto it, throw the coat over and put on the silly shoes, downstairs on the elevator, the ramp, Ke Karlovu, by the two hospitals, like Mrs. Müller, like any of the local nurses, nobody will notice, then, two houses later, quickly to the right in the direction of the steps, and then to throw him out from the wheelchair like trash from the can. Down the steps. Then a complicated thing again: she's got to hide the wheelchair at the top end of the steps for a few minutes, or simply conceal it in the bushes, run down the steps, prop the unmoving body against the post, tie it with the same cord she'd used to choke him, quickly run back up the steps, and then calmly ride the empty wheelchair to the hospital. Leave it with dozens of others. Then quickly back, to finish cleaning the apartment, take money out of the safe, and leave. Nobody'll ever know. Sweet revenge. And to have a memorial built up for the rich man's money to commemorate his victims. Justice is victorious. Simple Count of Monte Cristo. A Mexican series. Bollywood in all its beauty. And who said that life is something different? A city soap opera, all of us live in it. In the best case, *in* it, of course. Could be worse.

All right then, let it be this way. But the plot has to be perfected. Did she know Vladimir Ivanovich in Perm? Did she ever see him? Various details depended on it, but the chain has been created and it's no longer possible to break up the unwavering loop of its logic. But still, I wonder. I opened another window and typed "museum Perm sculpture." And here it is, funny that it didn't pop up the previous time: "Rubashkina, Sofia Nikolaevna, b. 1956, candidate of arts, specialized in Perm wooden sculpture, senior research fellow, author of the monography . . ." The list "1990s Staff" doesn't show when she resigned. Pity. I typed "Rubashkina Sofia Nikolaevna." Almost zero results, understandably. Only in the forums somebody retells the story of the daughter. A girl of ten years was sitting on a swing, a cord got wrapped around her neck, she choked herself. Stop. What choked herself? What girl? Whose girl? Lisa Rubashkina. Where were the parents? Why did they leave her without a guard? Oh yes, she's a Rubashkina. Of course. How could I make such a mistake? Two voiceless consonants — and such a pronounced difference . . .

It was a great plot, truly great. I'm sorry to let it go. By the way, to tell the truth, there was a weak link. Sofia didn't know where Okurov hid his money. She couldn't know. He used to open the safe without witnesses. Only once, when he was paying me for a collection of handmade stamps by the local conceptualists, he asked me to go out of the room and I secretly watched it all—he pulled away the small cabinet, quickly inserted his hand under the bottom of the TV receiver, a wide, flat drawer popped out, stacks were lying there like in American crime movies. I pretended I couldn't hear when he asked me to come back. He had to come out of the room and saw the art dealer closing the bathroom door behind him. Just to make sure. With these people one has to be careful.

She didn't know where the money was. I knew. Only I knew it, nobody else.

The Last Story

First I'm going to tell you something about myself, because the things that have recently happened to me are mysteriously and horribly connected to the story of my life, to the place and time in which I was born and grew up, to who my friends were, whom I loved, what I read. These things, the things we're made of, usually remain in the darkness; they're the walls of the soul; yes, you can feel them with your hands, but you cannot read the signs and charts of your destiny until somebody, whether yourself or another person, turns on the light and starts taking stock: he was born there, had such and such parents, studied, loved, made friends, read. And only when each—even the very last—brick of that wall is examined, will the soul be able to see its own personal *mene, tekel, parsin*. Or it won't see anything at all because it's hiding its head under its wing out of shame or fear—I mean, a soul's got to have wings, right?

I was born almost forty years ago in a proletarian district of a proletarian city. Flesh of the flesh of the country and the time, I was living the life given to me, living it in the pre-determined limits of my childhood, boyhood, and youth. My parents got divorced and I went to live with my grandpa and grandma as a temporary solution, and wound up there permanently. They belonged to an educated class; it wasn't surprising then that from a very early age, I subconsciously did my best to become friends with the little proletarians, putting them—hardy and merry little boys in their shirts buttoned on the first button—on a rather large pedestal, almost a stage, on which they were playing their never-ending games: they drank alcohol smuggled into the school, smoked cigarettes, ate fried sausages with potatoes, went to the military area to collect cartridges, and played cards. I did the same things, but in a somewhat stilted manner, as if putting all those wonderful activities in quotation marks, citing them.

That's how I spent the first years at my school, which was a typical example of the Soviet authorities' extravagance during the "enlightenment" period—it specialized in the English language, ergo it was an elite school, but its pupils were the offspring of the simplest families, living in the neighborhood. The son of a factory deputy head and a cleaning lady's daughter shared the same desk. A full socialism, except that English was spoken there six lessons a week. In the eighth year, we covered the desks with lines from songs by Queen and in the ninth, we analyzed a story by Hemingway with our teacher. However, all that was happening under the reign of the proletarian spirit and we were also familiar with the stories of the local underworld.

How did I spend those years? Well, in almost exactly the same way as everybody else. I idled at all lessons except English, smoked Laika and Prima cigarettes in the bushes at the schoolyard (oh, those unforgettable boyish discussions, those comments on the nonexistent sexual life, those precise definitions of the guitar licks of our beloved Blackmore and Page, those rude and gentle dreams about our future, in which the Nabokovian mixed with the Platonovian!), chased the ball at the Summer Sports Stadium, gulped down the sticky Solntsedar wine, hugged my sweaty female classmates with the melancholy *Welcome to the Machine* playing in the background, rebelled, driving grandpa and grandma to their graves, kicked the fallen leaves in the Adventure Park of an indescribable decadent beauty, regularly visited action films with fat-lipped Belmondo, suffered and fretted, hoped, envied, read tons of books about war history, sadly ignoring Turgenev and Gorky, whom the school was trying to force upon me, was beaten up by the gang from the Northern Estate, beat up the gang from the Northern Estate, leafed through the exciting Yugoslavian magazines, with merry blondes' pink tits springing up from their pages, fretted, envied, imitated, envied, suffered. There were other things too, but I can't remember now. My memory has retained mostly sounds, smells, and colors; events didn't form into plots, they got lost in the accounting books of life. How I hoped they'd got lost forever!

Having got rid of the school troubles, I boldly stepped into the university trouble, which was markedly different. I managed to turn my strange hobby of the school years—passion for the musketeer wars of the seventeenth century, for the great Turennes, Condés, Wallensteins, and Princes Rupert—into the topic of my diploma thesis, the defense of which proved to be extremely easy. On the whole, studying at the Faculty of History was easy and even pleasant. The Soviet authorities didn't spare money on this type of education, albeit superfluous and wholly unnecessary from their point of view. Thus for the courses of Latin, Greek, history of antique clothing, and Winckelmann's aesthetics, I had to pay a rather symbolic price of two or three funny subjects the likes of "scientific communism" and "the basics of counterpropaganda." I felt comfortable at the university. The drinking and smoking, which was a must there, could've turned me into a proper troublemaker but, as I'd always kept a little distance, I preferred to remain an observer rather than to indulge in unrestrained rioting; I was always cordial, respectful, and ready to share the common enthusiasm, but not for long—not forever. I walked the faculty corridors with the look of a person who's got a firm intention to see a few other places in his life. Oh no, it wasn't a lowbrow Romantic affectation, I wasn't Lermontov's Pechorin with his "what is that to me, a travelling officer," God forbid! There was something else, so far unknown to myself; I was the tipsy gentleman, who was capable of drinking away his not-snowy-white shirt, and of shaking off the cops. However, as soon as I came back home and had a bath, I turned into a man who read Machiavelli and Comte de Saint-Simon, understood the lines of Coleridge and Chesterton in original, and loved a good discussion about Gnostics with the half-blind old woman from the Department of Classics. That same old woman, as it became clear years later, had spent the twenties in Petersburg; she'd been friends with Bakhtin and Yegunov, and had even got to see Kharms. Yes, I liked the university.

The girls there were of a fun kind too. I avoided the silly dorm licentiousness, as well as "princesses" with a smoky voice and interesting past (usually including the clap and a few abortions). I liked the normal ones, who united a provincial common sense with the similarly provincial dreaminess, and were seriously looking for something new. For their sake, it was possible to embark on adventures, and make plots happen; discussions with these almost perfect ladies inflamed my blood: there wasn't a moment of boredom or obscenity! Only one thing didn't work out—by the last year almost all of them had got married. But I wasn't bored as I had a most fearful occupation during that year. I moved out of my grandparents' house, making extra money by teaching lessons in an evening school for the clothing industry workers (all female), in that refined communist brothel which was paying me, the client, for the received sex; I was writing my diploma thesis, finishing reading some important books, so that I wouldn't have to open them ever again in my life. And of course, music—punk, new wave, avant garde—which I loved, oh how much I loved it! And never listened to it since.

With the diploma in my pocket, I was spit out into the destitute world of the early perestroika. It was disgusting. You see, I'd planned it all in advance: PhD, dissertation about the Thirty Years' War, a pleasant, unburdening associate professorship, regular bachelor life in my own one-room apartment, a somewhat idle libertinism, books, films, music. I had enough money too—a friend from the "Knowledge" society found me a position in a group of traveling lecturers on any and all topics; we were supposed to enlighten inmates and their guards in prisons of various security levels that could be found in the hidden corners of our region. The job paid well, much better than the lessons for the clothes-sewing girls, and the visits themselves, including their special rooms full of propaganda materials and Lenin rooms, were interesting too. Yes, I'd really planned it all in advance, there was just one thing I hadn't foreseen—the end of the period.

At that time, as it seemed to me (and as it seems now), we were having stinky gray weather, with mud in the streets, either the beginning of November or of April. Hesitating for a couple more years, I took a deep breath of the still relatively clear air and dived deep, so deep that I emerged on the other side, in the other world, and not even quite myself. Those years, crowned with bunches of ration coupons for flour, democratic leaflets, and portraits of the last secretary general, floated by on the surface, just like a couple of following years, chaotic and monotonous. I was lying low in my yellow submarine in Avtomekhanicheskaya Street, not perceiving anything, gulping down in turns bread and vodka, writing my dissertation. I was reading newly published old books, having given my TV to the hapless lady doctor who'd played the main role in the awkward pantomime of the quick breakdown of my marriage. I emerged no sooner than at the beginning of October 1993, although the word *emerge* would better describe my first dissertation opponent, a Moscow professor by the name of Z. A sweet person and a winter swimmer, he emerged from the Ostankinsky lake in Moscow exactly on the day when the fanatical crowd set out to destroy the nearby TV tower. They considered the naked Z a counterrevolutionary, tied him up, and threw him in prison, from which they released him in a week, equally naked. That is, they didn't release him but carried him out — to the mortuary, from there to the civil funeral at the university, and then to the cemetery. At my dissertation defense the poor Z was replaced by a randomly assigned cosmopolitan deconstructivist X, who, regardless of the obvious lack of connection between my Hapsburgs and his Baudrillard, turned out to be a nice guy, and at the graduation banquet wrote down on a napkin the telephone number of his friend, who was working at the humanitarian fund established by a certain idealistic philanthropist, may God protect his stock exchange rates. So that's how I emerged. The philanthropist, a sentimental Czech, had escaped to the States back in 1968 and made a few billions of dollars on something deadly. Thus he presented his homeland with a special historical institute and made it its mission to summarize in detail the mournful Bohemian and Moravian past. So I got a job with them — setting in order the deposit of Jesuit treatments about the nature of the country and working reports on the annihilation methods used against Czech Protestantism. So, thanks to the rebellion of the Soviet revanchists, police brutality, the kindness of an accidental deconstructivist, and the patriotism of a Czech émigré, I found myself in Prague, deceiving the destiny that seems to be waiting for me at the corner of my native Avtomekhanicheskaya Street.

Here, with a few years' delay, I received all that I'd planned for myself on graduation. And a little more than that. I spend six pleasant hours a day in the long extension added to the Jesuit hospital in the Kateřinská Street: I sit there, unhurriedly analyzing some prior's extremely neat handwriting, attributing his citations to Saint Augustine and Thomas Aquinas, scanning, translating the texts into a dry nonexistent English I've made up myself to convey the messages of the empty seventeenth-century Latin. How sweet it is to convert the remnants of the Soviet education, received free of charge, into real money! Even the course on the basics of counterpropaganda came in handy—that's what the Jesuits were doing in these lands, after all ... My life has thus found its own course—instead of a one-room apartment in a tower block, I have a *garsónka* in Prague, of the exact same size, but much more comfy, in a nineteenth-century house with tall walls, located in the Žižkov district, gloomy and decrepit in a Romantic way. I walk to work through a funny park on a hill, from which you can see the whole city, bristling with spires, then go down, turn left and right, then downwards again, and here I am—my table with neat piles of dictionaries and reference books, an open incunabulum, a computer, and a cup of green tea. Through the window I can see the large hospital park, families are walking their ill, orderlies are smoking at the small door, heavy branches of chestnuts are hanging above. The autumn is well underway. It's here that I was waiting, but why such a plaintive tone! here I *am* waiting for death, tranquil, confident, undisturbed. Perfectly undisturbed, if it weren't for one particular circumstance, but later about that.

I adore this city, but I can hardly stand its village-like inhabitants—unwashed men with beer bellies, curvy girls with wide cheekbones who take every opportunity to expose their flanks, drugged homeless, nasty old women, dried up in their chase for an extra crown—all these characters are foreign to the city of Prague, and it's by pure accident that they've inherited one of the architectural miracles of Europe. But, I've got to give them credit for one thing— they don't molest me with any strong feelings. All they're capable of is durable enmity towards the foreigner. It satisfies me.

I spent about five to six years organizing myself. I was learning the local speech, ringing with the *r-zh* sound, meeting people,
establishing romantic relationships, observing the city, the country,
the neighboring countries. I didn't go to visit my homeland, and
hardly ever phoned, because I had nobody left there, except a few
old friends. Just for the fun of it, I signed up for the email newslet-
ter of my native N-sk and usually started my working day reading news about fires that had flared up through the fault of some
drunken smoker, about sport contests of disabled children, about a
heated city budget discussion, about a festival of folk crafts and the
victories of the local hockey players. It was here that on one beautiful autumn morning, may it be damned, I came across the name of
Konstantin Svistkov for the first time.

The headline of the article of the InfoSite agency said: "FEL-
LOW TOWNSMAN KONSTANTIN SVISTKOV'S *ON THE
PILGRIM'S ROAD* SHORTLISTED FOR RUSSIAN BOOKER
PRIZE." An eye-catcher here—the wild whistle in both the first
and last names of the author and the title of his book, at first sight
sanctimoniously Orthodox, but in fact a literal translation of Bunyan's *The Pilgrim's Progress*, diluted with sweaty provincial Kerouac,
and the sweet provincial thrill caused by the literary success of the
fellow townsman . . . I laughed and started working on my Jesuits.
At lunch I again remembered the pious whistler. In the evening I
couldn't restrain myself any longer and typed "Konstantin Svistkov"
into the search box of the omniscient Yandex.

It's not that I'm not a reader. On the contrary, I am a reader
and an experienced, earnest, and grateful one. My knowledge of
literature isn't distinguished by width but by depth. Having once
conquered Joyce's one-day epic, I delightedly became a member of
the sect of his worshippers, not avoiding even the most exaggerated
signs of love, up to the journey to Dublin to take part in the somewhat ad-like Bloomsday pilgrimage. I still want to heap up a few
months of holiday and dedicate it to the translation of a few pages
of *Finnegans Wake* into Russian. After all, Joyce's fleeting mention of
the Irish general who died in 1620 near Prague (and I know exactly

where it happened! at the White Mountain!) has inspired in me the idea to create the biography of O'Riordan from Connaught, who'd fought under Waldstein's flag at first, and then under Prince de Condé's (I hope to offer this work to the reader in a few years' time). Having grasped Joyce, I picked up the ever-changing O'Brien, misanthropic Beckett, and simplistic Kavanagh. I always adored two other Irishmen: Swift and Wilde. My knowledge of the literary space beyond the borders of the Emerald Isle is much humbler. I prefer Larbaud to Céline, fell asleep over Thomas Mann, woke up over Musil, I'm always ready to trade the talkative Durrell quartet for any story about Jeeves and Wooster. I know Russian literature well, but haven't read anything more recent than Sasha Sokolov. Wait, no; a couple of years ago an acquaintance from Petersburg sent me something that didn't bore me to death. I liked that.

And so, putting on an old-fashioned pair of Joyce-like spectacles, I peeked behind the internet subconscious of contemporary Russian letters. If I'd done it just so, out of a lazy curiosity—never mind then. I wouldn't have survived more than twenty minutes sitting in that Dostoyevskian honky-tonk: beards, flagons, hysterics, preaching, cockroaches on the wallpapers. But I was hunting my Kostya Svistkov, so I quickly walked from room to room, making a point of not looking right or left. I was leafing through site after site, clicking on link after link, until I noticed the name of my pilgrim townsman in a critical article. A fiery-eyed (if we're to believe the photo) man of the name Yegegeyev was discussing the Russian Booker prospects on the site *Belledejour.ru*. The content of the article corresponded to the title of the column, "Practical Peristaltics of Thinking," in a strangely appropriate manner. Yegegeyev was writhing; drowning in his own stinking clouds, he maligned authors and their works, instigating the crowds to follow the great traditions of psychologism and reflection of the truth of life, hazily pledged allegiance to democracy and common sense, maligned again, this time rather insolently, until finally, he was ripped apart by the sounds of his own peristalsis. I had to twice run my eyes through this image of the self-declared physiologism, to discover what I'd been looking for: "Having seen the list of the Booker laureates, of course, I froze. If you dig very deep in the overflowing shelves of my memory, you certainly can find a case when I didn't know some name in the shortlist at all. You will understand that I cannot read everything! But now—*three* names! Dear me! Three! And I definitely don't know them! Nonsense. Who are all these people? What kind of animal is Perepletov? In what waters is Dolphinskaya swimming? Not mentioning Svistkov. It is theoretically possible that an author, unknown to me, suddenly started giving birth to masterpieces. But in that case, somebody should have passed the message on to me. No. I definitely don't remember anything like that, nobody ever lectured on the works of Perepletov, Dolphinskaya, and Svistkov." After these fireworks, Yegegeyev moved on to the analysis of the works of the guilty shortlisteds: "Svistkov's *On the Pilgrim's Road* is a product of futile scribbling. He is an imitator who doesn't have the faintest idea that the goal of literature is not literature per se, but 'I,' of course I don't mean me, Yegegeyev, but the likes of 'I'—people. That is, I, and those who live with me in the reality, outside literature. And if Svistkov is inside literature and I am outside it, then *On the Pilgrim's Road* is typical literature per se, to which I deny the right to be Real Literature."

This amazing Yegegeyevianism caught me unprepared. I thought that *On the Pilgrim's Road* would be a nice provincial prose in the Leskovian line, maybe with a jab of Salinger; but it seems, judging by the intensity of critical vapors, it's something completely different, because "literariness," as bearded critics tend to imagine it (I still remember something!), has an exclusive relation to foreign images, various Kafkas and Borgeses, but the "truth of life" is always on the side of epigones of Leskov, Tolstoy, and Boborykin. It means I was completely wrong, suspecting my fellow townsman of an accidental instance of plagiarism of the Bunyanesque title. It means there's a game there. The life of our N-sk doesn't spill over with games or at least not with clean games, so I involuntarily felt some affection towards Svistkov and his work. Later I came across two or three more reactions. Articulate Nina Donutenko told the author off for "strenuousness" and "misleading deceit": "Generally, the whole picture is over-complicated, the author is at times crying, at times laughing, but all of it sounds forced; he is slithering inside his book reality and expects us to find the answers to his literary questions. But we won't! That's not our job!" Now I got seriously angry, deciding that Svistkov must have created something Al-Mu'tasim-esque, Pierre-Menard-ian (the annoying Donutenko style!), something that in my opinion one shouldn't be doing. But the next literary lady told off the writer for following completely different paragons ("What will the familiarity with this novel give us? Don't we know Irving W.? I read *Rip Van Winkle* way back at the Institute of Literature!"), another reviewer praised him for a "conceptually faithful usage of discursive practices in the area of a full Oedipiality"; finally—and by now I was digging deeper and deeper, into the very undergrowth of this witches' reservation—the jury declared their decision, my Svistkov came out with nothing, and the first prize went to writer Sidorov for his novel *Ivanov*.

A double failure: my fellow townsman didn't get the prize and I didn't find any information about the content of his creation. I'd already put this story out of my mind, the more so because the usual depressing winter came to Prague, from which I'd had to save myself by short trips to Tangier and Cairo for several years. A week spent around there is a strong antidote against the visual avitaminosis, increased by the eternal image of the gray, decrepit walls of the Old Town and the similarly gray, similarly decrepit sky above them. I'd started saving the money for the trip well in advance, arranged the week off half a year before, and nothing could've prevented me from spending the end of February in one of the former Arabic caliphates. But two weeks before my departure, I came across a small article about *On the Pilgrim's Road* on the website of some half-philosophical magazine.

The article was written, most likely, by a philologist: a large part of the text was dedicated to the Bunyanesque subtext of Svistkov's novel. In the opinion of its author, the novelist tried to construct his work "above" Bunyan's allegorical narrative; the English paragon leads his hero, heading for the Celestial City, through places of cruel suffering and deadly sins—through the Vanity Fair, the Slough of Despond, and the Valley of the Shadow of Death; the N-sk writer drags his autobiographical hero, Kostya S., through areas of "distraction" (based on Pascal)—Sex, Alcohol, Friendship, Family. Each chapter of *On the Pilgrim's Road* is dedicated to one of these areas. Bunyan's hero reaches the Celestial City, but only in a dream; Svistkov's Kostya liberates himself from the "distractions" and focuses on his unique soul a moment before he's accidentally shot by a drunken policeman. So, Kostya's the winner.

It was with a certain suspicion that I was reading this article. I'm not all that fond of stunning revelations of the true literary sources of other works because those are built on the assumption that the author is not an architect but just a skillful manipulator of ready-made building blocks; it isn't exactly civil of the critic to ascribe his own deficit to the writer. But in this article, the philologist hit the nail on the head. It further diminished my enthusiasm regarding the novel itself. But the end of the article was rather encouraging: "The hero's name is Konstantin, the same as the name of one of the two saints who gave us the alphabet, letters, literature.[16] Kostya from *On the Pilgrim's Road* gives letters to the period he lives in, he articulates it. Starting in chaos, chapter by chapter, he is gradually purified and discards the generational, social, and national burden. Plunging himself into the context, more precisely—being born from context, he plays the role of a chemical substance from the action of which this context breaks down and falls on the world like rain. *On the Pilgrim's Road* is created on the intersection of two first novels of Joyce and the epic of Proust; but it is not about the formation of the 'artist' through 'finding the time' or breaking away from his time (and homeland); it is about the *articulation of time.*"

Yes, the solemn finale made me happy. From the comparison with Bunyan alone I'd guessed the *Ulysses*-like construction of *On the Pilgrim's Road* and the end of this article confirmed it. It seemed that my fellow townsman made a "cross-section of the period," so to speak, but not with naturalistic-scientific goals in mind as much

---

[16] St. Constantine-Cyril and Methodius created the first Slavic alphabet in the ninth century and codified the Old Church Slavonic language.

as to show the colorful image in yet another light. The exit of the country from the period named and articulated in the book was marked by the hero's death, and why not? Death is a new birth, after all. Not exactly an original idea, but one that works every time.

Something just poked me in the ribs. Judging by the biographical data uploaded to the Booker site, writer Svistkov is my peer. That means, he must have "articulated" my own period! I started to read the reviews and gradually piled up a bunch of details, clearly showing that Svistkov described my hometown, region, school, and faculty. Somewhere among the voiceless crowd of quotations from the book, I actually caught a glimpse of a few secondary characters from my own life. It seems that the author and I have acquaintances in common. Could our paths have crossed? I strained my memory, trying to dig up some buried Kostik, Kostyan, Kostas, Kostyukov- ich, Svistok, Svistonov . . . No. If I know this person at all, he must be hiding under a pseudonym now.

It was now impossible not to read the book, but it wasn't that easy to lay hands on it. There are a few places in Prague that sell Russian books but those are of such a quality that it would be better if they weren't sold at all. The online bookshops of my homeland had never heard of this city. I don't know anybody who'd be shuttling between the Czech Republic and Russia. Finally, three days before my flight to Tangier, I decided to take the most desperate measure—I set out to enroll in the Slavic Library in the Clementinum and there, after just a few steps with the brand-new reader's card in hand, my eyes were pierced by a modest blue book, standing on the shelf of new acquisitions. The book's title was *On the Pilgrim's Road*.

I didn't sleep that night. I read the novel twice—not because it's that good; although, I must admit, it's not bad at all. But I was re-reading it for another reason—because IT WAS WRIT- TEN ABOUT ME. There was no doubt about it. Svistkov knew my life down to the smallest details, in some points the images in our minds differed but the varying particulars could be put down to basic memory malfunctions. And more than that—the damned writer knew a lot of things that I'd been intentionally forgetting for a number of years!

For example, that scoundrel described in detail and with an obvious pleasure the scene of our last family scandal, which resulted in my parents' divorce: father's dull roar, mother's squeaking hysterics, my unhappy grandfather running out of my parents' room with his ears covered, his eyes large and brimming with tears, myself, a four-year-old tot, who'd intruded with a just-finished drawing of a tank decorated with a big red star, through the door that was ajar; I heard a wild yell, I don't even know whose it was, but it was undoubtedly addressed to me: "Out! Get out!" A swift slap and I come flying out of the chamber of horrors, sprawl on the opposite wall, and land on the floor, everything's floating in my eyes, my ears are ringing, the clean yellow wallpaper is quickly turning red, grandma is bustling around with a wet towel . . .

How did Svistkov find out about the greatest passion of my childhood and boyhood—toy soldiers? Apart from two or three friends, I never shared this secret with anybody: the world of the thousands of my paper warriors—pictures cut out from books, then glued to cardboards and carefully equipped with a folding base. Almost half a chapter from *On the Pilgrim's Road* is dedicated to the description of how the thirteen-year-old hero plays out the Napoleon 1806 campaign in the empty summer apartment, how, polishing the floor with his knees, he measures with his elbow the distance between the Prussians and the French, how he rejoices, putting the paper army of Count of Hohenlohe to flight, running to the next room, which represents the village of Auerstedt, where he—in the name and on the order of Marshal Davout—shatters the divisions of the Duke of Brunswick; how finally, when the parallel victories had been won and all that was left was to unify the victorious French army and lead it to the kitchen, onto Berlin, the front door opened and my grandparents came in, returning from the cottage unexpectedly, you'd better do some serious work, you're playing pick-up sticks again, better read something for school, didn't buy any bread either, what a lazy bum of a boy.

And so, story after story, one more complicated and mortifying than the other, the damned novelist drags his hero, I mean, he drags me! to the concluding shot, which indeed seems like a salvation after all those horrible things that have happened to him. Svistkov collected almost everything that I knowingly let be forgotten. It was awful to remember it now, especially all together. He wrote a different version of my life, as likely as my own, but full of chaos and humiliation. The most terrible thing about it was that I didn't know who was to blame for this despicable deed, who didn't spare efforts and years to collect all these stories and then used them to patch up a novel! Who? I spent the rest of the night going through the few characters of my rather boring biography. Did anybody mess with literary creation? Was anybody known as a spy? Did anybody show any familiarity with John Bunyan's works? No, no, and almost no. I never had writer friends, avoided graphomaniacs like the plague, and my close friends from the N-sk period definitely preferred music to literature. The Bunyan part was more difficult — I did hang around with philologists at some point, especially those who majored in English; anyway, they're not the only ones who have to know the author of *The Pilgrim's Progress*, since Pushkin's *The Wanderer*[17] is studied by everybody. But none of those philologists I was friendly with was ever noted as an author. Moreover, the majority quietly went and sat down at bank offices and ministerial departments, firmly forgetting the difference between Bunyan and Benjamin. Spies? Such as would sniff out the details of my existence? Hardly, the more so because I usually don't carry the circles of friends from one period of my life over into another . . . But why not? The fateful novel tells only about my N-sk life . . . the longer I thought about it, the firmer I was in my conviction that Svistkov, for some reasons I didn't know about, spied on me with the help of my old friends — Penguin, Gloomy, Chief, Screechy, and who else could've told him about my parents, about the toy soldiers, about the pink satin bra of Lidka Krasavtseva, about the money stolen from the teachers' room, about how almost all my university accomplices hated me, and finally about how, in my fifth year there, I couldn't get out of a prolonged drinking bout and was taken to the

---

[17] A free translation by Pushkin of a part of Bunyan's *The Pilgrim's Progress*.

Lyakhovo lunatic asylum, from where my grandpa got me in the
end, calling upon his old connections. I've got to find the scribbler
and . . . and . . . and we'll see. We'll see. The important thing is to
find him.

I canceled the tickets to Tangier and went to my homeland instead—to search for Svistkov. Upon landing in Moscow, I started
from a visit to the Doppel-G press, which had published *On the Pilgrim's Road*. I never liked the capital, I never knew it well, and hadn't
been there for nine years, so this forced pilgrimage about its streets
presented for me, a sworn provincial, real suffering. The haughty,
vulgar, wretched Moscow, a gigantic village, into which billions,
dozens of billions of dollars have poured by accident, that city stank
unbearably—of the exhaust gases, the alcoholic breath of the red-
faced cops, Orthodox popes' oil, whores' perfume. It smelled both
physically and metaphysically; burying my nose in a handkerchief,
I, like a British soldier under Ypres, felt my lungs tearing apart,
along with my soul. But I reached the publishing house alive. After a short conversation with the secretary, I found myself in the
editor in chief's office. A tall young man, resembling a huge worm,
was falsely smiling at me and responded to my questioning with
a certain suspicion, which was in fact fully justified. I introduced
myself as a translator into Czech, and told him that I was interested
in Svistkov's work. Yes, first novel. No, we are the rights holder; if
you're interested, I can have a talk with the foreign rights direc-
tor. All right, we're fine with this, just find a Czech publisher. Yes,
pseudonym. No, we cannot disclose the author's real name, that's
how he wanted it. The worm started to overhang the table, unroll-
ing in all his wondrous length. If you're successful, get in touch,
here's my business card. The editor in chief deigned to walk the
visitor to the door, opened it, and suddenly guffawed with his hol-
low voice, leaned low next to my ear and said: "Actually, we don't
know his name. You see, we don't pay fees for the first books, so he
took his fifty author's copies and disappeared. I'd like to find him
now myself, we could publish his second novel. We'll give him four
hundred dollars. So, if you happen to find him, let him know. *Au*

revoir." Out in the street, I realized I'd forgotten to ask what their nameless author looks like. Damn. But I'd found out that there's a second novel.

I had nothing more to do in Moscow, and so I set out for my hometown N-sk with a light heart. My little homeland welcomed me with a pitiful February sun, dirty snowdrifts, and a somewhat chaotic, Yesenin-like atmosphere. Half-drunken men were wandering in lopsided mink-fur caps around the station and enjoying an inventive swearing shootout with their stately missuses (red lipstick, gold earrings, iron teeth). Loud and ugly music was pouring from the kiosks, probably composed especially for such occasions. Into the shuttle van, which I took to get to my Avtomekhanicheskaya Street, stepped a deadly-pale lieutenant with a bottle of beer held before him, and when the driver refused his ten-ruble payment with the words: "Veterans free of charge today!" it dawned on me—it's February 23, the Red Army Day. This circumstance was in line with my plans—to ask questions of my old friends in a relaxed atmosphere, with a glass in hand, take them while they're still warm, find out everything about the novelist scoundrel, spy, violator of the copyright convention concerning the private life, forger who'd swapped my biography for one that's also mine, but different. The culprit must be found and punished. Amen.

Five calls were all it took to find the drinking bout with the greatest concentration of the potential sources of information. Grasping a bunch of flowers, a bottle of *Becherovka*,[18] an obligatory present from a Prague guest, and a local half-liter bottle with the literary inscription "Recommended by Arina Rodionovna,"[19] I went to celebrate the holiday of the brave soldiers.

My heart was beating and roaring, but not from the expectation of the meeting with the dear comrades of my restless youth and merry prime, no doubt aged, worn-down, and duller than before. Not at all. I am free from such sentiments, that is—I've freed myself from them on purpose, in order to prevent myself from becoming an involuntary character in a collective novel. I alone create my bonds, the bonds to get nostalgic about when I go through them,

[18] An herbal liqueur produced in the Czech Republic.
[19] Arina Rodionovna was the nanny of Alexander Pushkin.

depending on my mood: a friend with whom I sat on the potty in the nursery, a fleeting fellow drinker in the Petersburg Water Lagidze, a wholly imaginary Montenegro singer of Italian songs. No, I was worried about something else. How and what will I be questioning them about? in what pocket can I smuggle my questions into their midst? with what parachute should I later jump out from their slow zeppelin, thus cutting the spiderweb of their nostalgic stories? A long memory is worse than syphilis, to be sure. Whistling a song from our communal past, I rode up to the fourth floor of a shabby panel house in the Street of Hero Komarov, which is perpendicular to Lenin Avenue and parallel to Krasnodontsy Boulevard.

In a small darkish room were sitting half a dozen youngsters grown old in the company of women of various ages. They were drinking. I recognized my friends immediately, but the palette of their helpmates had fully changed in nine years. Penguin is still grinning in a kind and lazy way into his herb-scented beard. Chief's bald head has the same shine, and the lonely ham sandwich is once again missing company on his plate. Kiryan crowns his own jokes with his old squeaky guffaw, arranging his glasses with his index finger. Gorky reaches out for the bottle with the same graceful movement. On the table are the unchanging, traditional Soviet Olivier salad, and mushrooms with pickled cucumbers. Here's Swift Bill pricking his fork into a slimy milk-cap ... I froze; it suddenly seemed to me that all those years hadn't passed, and I hadn't gone anywhere, it was as if I'd dreamed it all up in the middle of this timeless drinking bout—Prague, Jesuits, unhurried walks around the Vinohrady district, pilgrimages to Vienna and Berlin, the hard labor of my alcohol-and-tobacco abstinence, my Irish studies. As if I'd been born here, between the fork and the glass, with the wailing of Tom Waits in the background, and here's where I'll die too. I'll be wrapped in a sheet and placed in the next room, and then they'll continue their unhurried worship of the Holy Trinity: Vodka, Canapé, Music.

They recognized me so quickly that I didn't have time to run away. They addressed me with the ancient nickname, tied me up, and threw me onto the sofa. They brought me a glass, a fork, and a plate, introduced me anew to all the svetas, natashas, marinas and zhannas; thank God I managed to stop Gorky, who'd intended to pour me the welcome glass, and had already grasped the bottle with his legendary gesture and the eternal exclamation of "The Hand of the Lord saved the Fatherland!" To refuse the drink was surprisingly easy: the petrifying word "cirrhosis" had already found its ground in our circle. I'd learned by heart the story of my Czech life before, so they left me alone in half an hour, and returned to the evaluation of the latest King Crimson album.

But my mission failed too. No matter how hard I tried—to nail it with a reference, to poke them with a joke, to pin it with a comparison, to amaze with a direct push: nothing worked. Nobody knew anything: not about the novel, not about its author, not about any spies sniffing out the shittiest details of my life. Nothing. Nobody read anything, nobody heard anything, nobody's interested in anything except vodka, milk-cap, and the latest King Crimson. Seeing me to the door, Penguin slapped me on the shoulder and said: "You, you come here more often, right?" Right, I promised, and ran down the stairs, never to return.

I had five days left before my departure. I hadn't walked the N-sk streets this much even when I'd lived here. I visited the sterile office of the "InfoSite," where a nice and bashful young man with an amazingly ugly face spent half an hour telling me about his meeting with novelist Svistkov, about how long his hair is, how he stutters, how slyly he speaks, how well he cooks, until I realized that this wolf of information was mistaking Svistkov for the writer Sorokin, who'd appeared on TV the night before in a cooking show—long-haired, stuttering, and sly, he had deftly roasted fish in the oven. I went to see Gloomy in his car-servicing workshop, but he didn't recognize me and I didn't start pounding my fist against my chest, saying I am such and such, your childhood friend, your classmate, do you remember how they beat us up at the dance in the park? I left. I talked to drunken Ogushkin in a dark corner of the company printing office, I had an audience with the deputy head of the department of external relations and social protection Peterpaulov, going by the nickname "Two in One"; a PhD friend Kimrov took me to the grave of poor Professor Zontikov. All in vain. Either there's a conspiracy against me in N-sk and somebody mean foresaw down to the tiniest variants the path of my pointless search for the nameless literary spy, or I became a victim of a monstrous, word-by-word, syllable-by-syllable congruence with Svistkov's novel. I preferred to believe the latter, in fact more unlikely than the former; so I went home to Prague. Three days after my return I read on the InfoSite news that a Svistkov literature evening with the author, including a reading and a banquet, had taken place in the N-sk Actor's Club.

I wrote to the journalist who'd brought to the readers the coverage of this excellent event in the cultural life of the city and he— after my lengthy persuasion and false confirmations of affection including equally false invitations to Prague—drew with his shaky pen a portrait of my fellow townsman writer. He's of average build, about 170–175 cm tall. Black hair, Harlem-like stubble. Glasses. Jeans. Light-gray polo. Silver ring on his left hand. Vigorous tenor. He told him about his childhood in Rostov-on-Don, in the Bratskiy Drive. His father—a soldier—brought him as a young man to study at the N-sk medicine school. He works as a homeopath in some huge multinational company. "Dear Sergey, thank you for the masterly description of Svistkov. Your literary talent is obvious. You have to start writing immediately, preferably a novel. As for your arrival in Prague, so much expected by me: I'm awfully sorry to tell you, the management are sending me on an urgent business trip to Paraguay—to analyze the local archive of the Jesuits who ran it there in the nineteenth century. As soon as I arrive in Asunción, I'll get in touch. All my warmest wishes! Yours . . ."

I gradually returned to my quiet life, measured by the precise vessels of Prague alchemists, to my conscientious Jesuits, to my witty O'Riordan, to my green tea, to my visits to Shakespeare and Sons, to the Japanese shop in the Korunní Street, to the weekly meetings with Madla, to the happy spending of the two decades that I had left until old age. I didn't forget about *On the Pilgrim's Road*—you can't forget something like *that*, no, rather, I put this story into one of the long drawers of my memory, somewhere next to the records of my unhappy marriage. Only I gained a nasty habit—once every few weeks I fleetingly leafed through Russian literary sites, cowardly persuading myself that I was doing it only for the sake of getting to know what was new in the realm of books.

The break lasted half a year—at the beginning of September my friend Svistkov gave an interview for the now fashionable magazine *Turn the Page*. I can't say that the son of a bitch was wholly un-witty—he sharply labeled the villains from the *Belledejour.ru*, call-ing them "peristaltic Pericles" and "soft-bread Ms. Pretzel." Svist-kov mentioned that he'd read Bunyan in the original during the torture of a Moscow-New York flight: very aptly, somebody'd left their PocketBook in the seat pocket among the advertising publica-tions and instructions about how to put on the oxygen mask. The uncompromising Protestant tinker moved the writer (who wasn't a writer yet), and he began to create a similarly guileless character. Svistkov decided to furnish him with an unhappy childhood, fully British whims of a young gentleman, heavy Russian inclination for vodka and exaggeration, and then started to describe the *dolce vita* at the end of the Soviet era in the character's own heavy style. The author didn't know what to do with him, Kostya S., in the post-Soviet period, so he supplied the novel with a drunken cop and his loaded gun. No, there's no Joyce or Proust, I couldn't even get myself to finish them. No. The writer W. was called *Ivlin* and the story of the sleeper was written up by Washington Irving. Yes, yes, the Columbia district. Nabokov? Used to be crazy about him, now his puns irritate me. A heavy joker. Read *Despair* recently. What a plot to spoil! By the way, I've just finished a new novella, the last story, I resurrected my hero and decided to send him into some half-imaginary place, some middle of nowhere; I was pondering it for a long time, hesitating between Aktobe and Asunción, until I remem-bered the Nabokovian Prague, deprived of all recognizable features. And I sent my dear hero to that Prague. Let him live a hermit's life for a little while . . .

I became physically sick from the blabber of that cheeky joker. He tore up my past, and he's now aiming at my present. I could picture what version of my local life Svistkov created, what low and filthy abysses he dug out under the harmonious, faultless mechanisms of my proud rituals! What a bunch of repulsive characters he unleashed upon my solitude! What pathetic, humiliating, ridiculous deeds he forced me to perform! I was sitting, glued to the edge of the table, my temples were throbbing in a wild jazz rhythm, my left shoulder was aching dully, my eyes were full of stars, planets, constellations, I found myself in an ambulance. Two orderlies in white uniforms were sitting on either side of the stretcher and with a kindly rebuke were staring at me. In order to secure my existence in this world, I tried to smile and moaned: *"Ahoj! Jak se máte?"*[20]

The next three weeks were dragging on long, grim, and silly. First I was lying in a tiny room and merry doctors brought their colleagues to look at my scar from a bullet one centimeter from my liver and I was telling them in my eloquent literary Czech how long-long time ago, a lawman was *trochu opilý*,[21] overly playful with his gun, and shot me right here. And a Russian lady doctor cured me. In that moment those stallions started neighing, saying that Russian doctors are *špatné*.[22] No! I whispered at the unbelieving crowd, not *špatni!*[23] Russian doctors are *héski!*[24] *Šikovný pán*,[25] they responded and disappeared. Then they brought me to a large room, where I spent days and nights on ether voyages. A colleague from the institute brought me a radio receiver. The more I splashed around in that purely non-material world, the more calmly I was remembering Svistkov and his works, after all, what's the difference between whether he copied my life or created it; even the fact that the son of a bitch reached with his filthy little hands here, to Prague, doesn't bear much consequence either, because I live earlier than he writes, I'm always ahead by a moment. And that's enough. I'm the master

[20] "Hello! How are you?"
[21] "a little drunk"
[22] "bad"
[23] "bat"
[24] "prettee"
[25] "Cool gentleman"

and he's just an interpreter of my will, my wishes and whims. I was deep in my soul-soothing contemplation, when, on a golden autumn day, the doctors decided that the patient was fully recovered, I packed my things and, staggering in the body of a stranger, I walked downstairs, marched through the magical hospital garden that I'd been greedily observing for the past two weeks, glued to the window, then I squeezed through a narrow door and went outside.

The following day I was already at work—quiet, kind, purified by the illness. As advised by a doctor, I brewed red Rooibos grown in the Antipodes instead of green tea, and sat down to my computer to check my emails. They were asking me to urgently send them material for a publication, announced new acquisitions of the British antiquarian booksellers, a Parisian institute based in Champs-Élysées was inviting me to an interesting conference about the baroque relation to death. *Pourquoi pas?* I didn't type in the browser line the news of N-sk anymore. But here's a message from them, not from them, it's from that journalist—what's his . . . Sergey?—who'd described Svistkov for me. I hesitated a little, but then opened the email. Well yes . . . dear . . . excuse . . . don't know where you're now . . . in Paraguay or . . . editor in chief heard about you and asked me to interview you . . . Our People Abroad section. Well damn, he took his chance. The arrow of the cursor trembled above the Delete button. Here's a P. S. I don't know if you're still interested . . . Svistkov . . . tragedy . . . died . . . his Lada with a truck . . . last story . . . if you want to read it, this is the link: www.swedenborg.ru/svistkov_last_story.

I clicked on the blue link, had a sip from my mug, leaned back in my armchair and started to read: "First I'm going to tell you something about myself, because the things that have recently happened to me are mysteriously and horribly connected to the story of my life, to the place and time in which I was born and grew up, to who my friends were, whom I loved, what I read. These things, the things we're made of, usually remain in the darkness; they're the walls of the soul; yes, you can feel them with your hands, but you cannot read the signs and charts of your destiny until somebody, whether yourself or another person, turns on the light and starts taking stock: he was born there, had such and such parents, studied, loved, made friends, read. And only when each—even the very last—brick of that wall is examined, will the soul be able to see its own personal *mene, tekel, parsin*. Or it won't see anything at all because it's hiding its head under its wing out of shame or fear—I mean, a soul's got to have wings, right?"

A String of Coincidences

The report of the expedition was submitted to the local institute of the Academy of Sciences on Thursday, April 27, 2006, in two forms—as a fat green folder with its corners tied by pink elastic bands, and as a PDF file. At first the institute's secretary had trouble opening it, but after some effort on her part and two calls to the IT person, she finally managed to open and save it under a more suitable filename. The secretary—a woman of advanced age who'd sacrificed her life, as she put it, to the "service of science," but ended up "left behind"—underwent all these operations at the very end of the working day and had already prepared to leave for a dinner she was having with a friend (an employee of a pharmaceutical company, likewise experiencing remorse with regards to an unrealized scientific career), when, accidentally glancing at the content of the green folder, she immersed herself in reading and was forced to change the booking of the restaurant table to a later time. She'd only seen about a quarter of the expedition's materials, and as she decided to examine the rest of it at home, she sent the electronic form of the report to her personal email address. Having done it quickly, the secretary closed the door of the office, handed the keys to the porter, and hurried to the restaurant, where she was expected by her friend, by this time slightly irritated. It was especially the speed of these operations that was the reason why she didn't see the provider's response—her inbox was full and the email containing the PDF file could not be delivered. At dinner, the secretary told her friend about the startling report and expressed her wish to return to scientific research now, when "late in years," and analyze the mystical phenomenon the expedition had discovered. Her partner in discussion expressed some doubt, noting that in the local institute of the Academy there will be people, who, as she poetically worded it, "wish to enter the Hall of Fame riding on other people's shoulders." The secretary couldn't but agree with this statement, but she remarked that she had a certain advantage—she partly knew the content of the report already and was planning to fully familiarize herself with it tonight. Having finished dinner with a cup of coffee, the friends parted and hurried home. The secretary's house was in a ten minutes' walk from the restaurant. She lived with her mother in a small apartment she'd bought after completing an excellent translation of a hugely popular novel *The Wonder of Mnemonics* by French writer P. Marcel for a commercial publishing house. The best translation of the year award enabled her to build her own Xanadu and acquire real property. The apartment was situated on the second floor of a modern four-story house, built next to a railway embankment, so she had two options to get home: she could either walk along a little bridge above the railway, or squeeze into the forbidden zone through a hole in the fence, and run across. She always made use of the other way, persuading herself that as she wasn't yet that old, she'd always be able to notice the approaching train and avoid death. That evening she must have encountered an obstacle, because in the morning of the following day, Friday, April 28, 2006, her mutilated body was found on the railway embankment.

At the same moment when the secretary, still alive, was finishing her gnocchi with mushroom sauce and washing them down with a glass of Soave, the guard of the local institute of the Academy of Sciences was pouring boiling water over his Chinese noodles and making ready to watch *The X-Files*. This old man, who'd left the army service with the rank of major, in his own words "adored science." Reading sci-fi books was his favorite pastime but he condemned sci-fi films for their inappropriate pretentiousness; *The X-Files* was almost the only exception to this. Every morning he took part in a lively discussion about the books he'd read and shows he'd watched with those employees of the Academy who shared his interests. The discussions usually ended on the observation that science still has a good deal left to explain. At the same moment when the agents Scully and Mulder were about to discover the nature of the amazing mnemotechnical abilities of a Canadian boy from the little town of Omemee, who remembered the travel of three-year-old Elvis Presley (accompanied by his parents) to New Orleans down to the smallest details, a short circuit occurred on the second floor of the academic building. The fire quickly moved to the still unopened stacks of books that were standing in the corridor—they were copies of the just-published memoirs of the Academy's late head dealing with the tempestuous sixties of the previous century. The guard only smelled the smoke after the fire had destroyed the whole second floor. He called the fire brigade and ran upstairs to close the heavy iron fire door that separated the first floor from the rest of the building. The subsequent investigation couldn't explain why he closed the door from the other side and stayed on the staircase, which the fire had reached by then. The firemen's arrival was considerably delayed because they'd had to wait for the maneuvers of a train on the railway crossing. As a result, the Academy of Sciences building burnt down to the ground. The following day at the extraordinary meeting of the municipal government, a decision was adopted to have a new, contemporary building constructed in the suburbs of the city in the Memorial Park district. The family of the guard received a huge compensation and insurance remittance, thanks to which the widow could at last move away from the daughter's family and buy her own small apartment on the second floor of a modern four-story house standing next to the railway. She was a little disturbed by the rattle of the passing trains that shook the house from ground to roof every two hours, but otherwise it was a perfect place to live in. The former owner of the apartment, a lonely woman who'd lost her only daughter in a tragic accident, had moved to a comfortable private retirement home, where the caring nurses, orderlies, and doctors are now in vain trying to fight the progress of Alzheimer's disease.

At the funeral of the secretary of the Academy of Sciences institute, the pharmaceutical company employee told her acquaintances about how, just a few hours before she died, her friend was very disturbed by the report of some expedition that had discovered a "place of memory" somewhere in the north of the country, at the heel of the so-called Twin Rocks. It seemed that with the approach of the night, every member of the expedition clearly saw places of their childhood and youth. The report was nothing other than a detailed description of those visions. What made this mysterious phenomenon so peculiar was that everybody only saw the places of his or her own past. The participants were most unwilling to share their stories and only when reminded of their duties to science and the funder, did they write up a report about what they'd experienced. Having received the money, the researchers left for their own countries and never showed any interest in the results of the expedition. Since the report itself was irretrievably lost in the fire, the management of the local institute decided to make inquiries of the management of the Academy. After a long exchange it became clear that the Academy had not commissioned any such research and had no information about any external funding of the same.

The Corner Café

He came to the café around eight o'clock every Tuesday evening. He enjoyed sitting there with a pot of disgusting tea or some nondescript beer, leafing through a local paper or a two-year-old issue of a magazine dedicated to alcohol and smoking. And of course, gazing out through the window. The café was located on the first floor of a corner house; his table stood in an acute angle created by two huge glass panels, so he could look both right and left—at the street leading to a square with a small park in the center, or at posters hanging here and there from the park's cast-iron fence, and the passing cars. In winter, it was already hopelessly dark at that time, and the headlights, the neon lights reflecting from the cars' glittering sides, and the random passersby flowing into the lit area around the café resembled all the favorite films of his youth at once, the films of Godard, Fellini, Truffaut, and Antonioni, those that had formed a background for such sweet dreams, dreams about foreign countries, solitude, love, freedom. He then found a similar place in Paris, either by the Luxembourg Gardens or at the Montparnasse Cemetery; rather, by the Luxembourg Gardens. A friend told him that it was in the local corner café—that is, in the *brasserie*, to use a more *chic* word for it—where Mastroianni had spent a few months, suffering from cancer and waiting for death. Where did Mastroianni die in the end? he mused, sitting in his glass corner, with his back to the bar, distractedly staring over the top of the newspaper at the evening sky, veiled in steel-gray mist. Thank God, it's summer now, July, so it's still light after eight in the evening, no romantic suicidal atmosphere around. No Godard. And Mastroianni is already dead.

His habit to frequent this place on Tuesday evenings arose as if by itself, but if he thought about it, the causes and consequences that had led him to the table in the café were so powerful that this result seemed to be the only one possible. It was Tuesday when it was his turn to do the broadcast and when that was over, it was impossible to even think of any activities other than a cup of tea. It was necessary to kill the rest of the evening, simply and mercilessly, overruling all objections, and thus he found this pleasant way of execution. The evening was being spent minute by minute and he was sitting, a withdrawn silent nobody, and with every gulp of tea or beer, every look in the window, every newspaper advertisement, he was sweeping out of himself the political trash which he'd collected so thoroughly during the first half of the working day to find a suitable place for it in the respective sections of his broadcast, and which he subsequently, during the second half, pulled out before the microphone and sent out floating on the medium, short, and ultra-short waves to various places of the Earth, silently longing for the moment when, at last, the red lamp on the studio desk would go out. "Good night!" were the words that put out the light; he collected his papers and pens, grasped an unfinished bottle of water, and found his way to his office through the dark, narrow corridor with studios on either side. Once there, he put his things away into the drawers of the writing desk, turned off the computer, put on (didn't put on) his coat, hung his bag over his shoulder and left. His movements mechanical, he did it all lightly and silently, like in a dream. He only woke up here, when saying one of his two usual lines to the waiter.

He never came here on other days and the square itself didn't lie on his usual paths through the city either, although it was only about fifteen minutes' walk from the house he lived in. However, on other days he didn't get so dead tired and he finished work earlier, and so in the evening he went for walks or to concerts, or simply stayed at home, read, listened to music, and prepared for his Sunday lesson of the local language. Yes, he lived a completely different life on other days, one that always left a little space for unfortunate literary creation, in which he'd been engulfed for the past fifteen years. He'd been told many times that he's a rather well-known author, that he has his own small readership, which, of course, may be smaller than the readerships of X or Y, but is smarter and more sophisticated. He didn't believe those tales at all, and not only due to modesty (for which his painfully low self-esteem passed off), but simply because it was only rarely that he came across any mention of

his own name in critical articles or in shortlists for the endless literary awards. His friends did tell him that he hadn't chosen the best
geographical position for success in his mother-tongue literature:
he left the capital of his country and of his literature, he left the
country too, but he didn't get as far as the capitals of exile writing,
where any mention of a street or a little park, fleetingly appearing
in a page of a book, guarantee acceptance into a great company of
writers; he didn't get far enough but settled in the middle, in a historical and cultural nowhere, generously strewn with architectural
decorations. The genres in which he (as even he believed) succeeded,
were foreign to his original literature. Moreover, his homeland ap-
preciated a high number of pages, cynical warmth or vice versa,
warm cynicism, whereas his works were distinguished for their brev-
ity, spare emotions, inclination towards play, and a certain naïvety
that couldn't be classified in any way. And so, his career as a writer
didn't work out extremely well, and he steadfastly remained at his
small literature works and genres. This didn't upset him too much,
because he looked upon his own work with a certain suspicion and
even disgust. Of course, at times he painfully yearned for fame, high
print runs, and, most of all, money, so much money that he could
leave his radio-factory job, stay at home, never having to follow the
news again, unhurriedly translate *Finnegans Wake* into his mother
tongue, write a contemplative journal, live a long life, die a quick
death. But to achieve that, he'd have to write wholly different books,
novels best of all, and he couldn't stand contemporary novels; as a
reader, he couldn't get halfway through them. No, he didn't complain about his life, it wasn't a bad life at all; in the repetition of the
everyday elements it consisted of, he saw the manifestation of that
great Order which was forever missing from the lives of his fellow
citizens, inclined more to the haphazard darkness of their native
Chaos. That's why he perceived his usual duties as rituals; it helped
him minimize the destructive effects the work had on his mind. As
for other duties and habits, those were simply pleasant and the most
pleasant of them all were his Tuesday evenings in the corner café.

These were the things he was playfully turning in his mind, sit-

ting at his table on a Tuesday evening in July. He'd already familiar-
ized himself with all the events of the provincial capital where he
was living, and read the review of a concert that was part of an aging genius's tour; the little teapot from which was hanging a thread
belonging to a bag of green Ahmad tea, had almost gone empty. He
decided to delay his departure as to allow the time for the streets,
which were still emitting heat, to cool down. The waiter changed
the teapot and brought him another local newspaper. It investigated
the shocking statement of a former secret service agent who said
that certain well-known grim fanatics had stayed in this boring city
thirteen years ago — literally three weeks before they destroyed two
world-famous skyscrapers in the sight of the whole planet. Why,
that would be fun. Would be. He was already living here at the time.
It's easy to imagine them standing next to him in the supermarket,
choosing between the local brands of sheep cheese and eating at the
neighboring table in a Turkish or Pakistani fast-food restaurant. Actually, if he turned his head right, and looked across the street, there
was a Pakistani fast-food joint. A wholly suitable place . . . Thrilled
with the slight possibility of joining History in retrospect, he began
to observe the joint more carefully. Nothing special. Five tables, a
bar counter with a cash register, and not a Pakistani of course, but a
real Arab standing behind it, there's a TV on the wall, he's probably
watching Al-Jazeera, green bands with sentences in an unknown
language are hanging all around, displayed on the window and fac-
ing onto the street are faded photographs of plates filled with curry,
bhuna, and samosa. If it weren't one of his innumerous rituals never to eat after seven in the evening, he'd have a look at their little
Islamist nest — to discuss the pressing matters of Jihad, although,
damn it, what can they possibly be, Sunnis? Shiites? The Arab came
out of the joint, closed the venetian blinds on the windows, returned and locked the door from inside. The second teapot was
finished, the waiter brought the bill, he left an extra coin as a tip,
you tip the waiter but a secret tip tipped the scales of power distri-
bution, let's walk on tiptoes as it's just the tip of the iceberg, Christ,
what nonsense, sleep, sleep, here's the passage, the apartment door,

shower, bed, getting up tomorrow at eight, no, at seven forty-five.

A week later, sitting at his table, he remembered how that night he'd dreamt about the joint. In his dream he was sitting inside, eating thick brown curry, and a dark-skinned man approached him and silently beckoned him to come and have a look through the tiny door next to the cash register. Over the man's shoulder he saw gray-bearded Osama bin Laden, dressed all in white, lying on a bed in the diminutive storage room; the man's eyes were looking at him kindly. One of his arms was naked and had catheters connecting it to a huge apparatus, which was standing at the head of the bed. Even in his dream he understood that it was a hemodialysis machine; the great terrorist suffered from a kidney disease. The door closed slowly and he returned to his curry, the taste of which he still felt on his tongue when he woke up in the morning. A startling dream. As usual, he twisted it this way and that, attempting to adapt it to his writing, but it didn't work. It hardly ever did with his dreams. And he immersed himself in an article that he already knew by heart about the production of the real, true, Madeira wine.

The next day, on Wednesday, he remembered his dream again. And what if bin Laden had really been hiding somewhere here, in this plain dreamlike country, in a place where nobody would ever dream to search for the leader of the worldwide Jihad? He began to think of reasons that could have led bin Laden to the pitiful little room in the local Pakistani joint and he only came to when almost the entire chain of events had been constructed. So, it all started a year before the fateful 9/11 . . . He took out a notebook and started to make notes. At the end of the second notebook he realized that he'd written up two chapters of a real novel. For the first time in his life he started a narrative from a distance, taking pleasure in describing the numerous secondary characters: the family members of the Saudi crown prince, double agents, barefooted Peshawar peasants with turbans on their heads, a blind Taliban mullah, and dozens of others. All this crowd didn't fit into a story or an essay anymore, all that was left was to pretend that he was writing just for the sake of it, for his own pleasure, just following his hand, although in fact there was a novel, an excellent novel budding in the notebooks, encompassing a lot of plotlines, pursuits, betrayals, descriptions of nature, scenes of battles and sex, and even containing some idea, no, not *some* idea but a whole bunch of rather consequential ideas, developing Tolstoy's historiosophy and Kierkegaard's existentialist philosophy at once.

Yes. A novel. He was now spending six days a week at work on the novel; he wrote in the evening during working days, and on the weekend he wrote in the morning and after his walk; he thought about the novel all the time and sometimes at work he turned his head away from the computer screen, looked out of the window at the Gothic spires of the gray Central European city, at the famous landscape on the other side of the river—the mountain with the castle standing on it, the spire of the cathedral rising high above, he looked with a long-forgotten pleasure, and suddenly, trying to remember the cause of that pleasure, delving into his mind for the reason why he was feeling so happy and festive, he remembered, yes, of course, he's writing a novel! Writing the novel was surprisingly easy, it didn't require any special effort regarding collection of the material, of the ethnographic, technical, and historical details; having worked at a political radio station for a few years, he knew by heart a big pile of sanguinary eastern events of the past three decades. The university education he'd received wasn't all that bad either, so all he had to do now was a little research on the internet or in an encyclopedia, or a call into the reading room of the library, in order to clarify the exact year of Daoud's overthrow. The only day when he didn't touch the novel was Tuesday. He took a rest from the novel on Tuesday: during the day he underwent the torture of the radio service, then sat in his café and stared out of the window, read newspapers and got lost in daydreaming. No, at first, during the early weeks, on Tuesday he observed the life of the Pakistani joint across the street, because it was there that the main plot of his novel, rich in plotlines, was centered, in the tiny room behind the tiny door made of white plastic. Now he knew exactly what that door was made of, just like he could imagine everything else—the rather dirty beige walls, the nickel bar, the huge fan under the ceiling, limply blowing about the air saturated with curcuma and coriander ... The joint was doing well and they'd taken on a new waitress, a dark little girl; swaying her full hips, poured into close-fitting jeans, she slowly shuttled between the kitchen and the tables which, as the autumn got closer, got more and more filled with the local Pakistanis, Arabs, and Turks in the evening, diluted with a few natives with a taste for hot aromatic food, and British tourists, instinctively having more trust in the former subjects of their own queen than subjects of some foreign emperor. He definitely liked the waitress: her figure, her rounded movements, her black headscarf, her large backpack she brought to work and left with late at night. He established that the girl probably studies medicine or law at the local university, and here's where she makes money to support herself. It was moving enough, especially when he remembered his own student life, in which there was no money at all, but the need for money wasn't all that great either. These are different times, he thought distractedly, he paid for his tea, left the tip, got up, put on his jacket, cast the last glance at the dark little figure with a notebook in her hand: chicken madras with jasmine rice, please, and a bottle of still water. The café had an exit on the right side, into the square; he had to walk along the house, the balcony on the second floor was always full of the staff of the local Jewish cultural center, they were smoking, pieces of their conversations reached his ears and, with a feeling of embarrassment, he remembered the unfinished book by Scholem every time, decorating his bedside table for half a year now, then he turned into a narrow little street where he always felt compelled to stop and look at the books displayed in the windows of a tiny esoteric press that had decided to release a series of mystical works in alphabetical order, Gurdjieff had been added to the collection in July and now, in September, Swedenborg. He crossed the large square with a neo-Gothic church, passed a sex shop on his right side, turned left, then left again, and there was the house he lived in.

As the novel progressed, his interest in the life of the Pakistani joint decreased. He'd almost stopped looking across the street, preferring to dream about the success of his future work. By day he remembered his visit to Frankfurt several years before; he'd seen huge banners hanging over the streets advertising a new novel of a phony Brazilian scribbler, who'd won over the hearts of office ladies. He decided that it was his name that was going to be on the banners next year. After all, his success is secured—by the disturbing topic, and the excellent style; he already knew that his almost-finished novel is written in a brilliant, outstanding way. On the last Sunday of November he wrote the last full stop. On Monday he, out of superstition, didn't touch his creation, only printed it, and on Tuesday he brought it to work with him. He decided to read the finished novel in one go especially on Tuesday, especially in his café, with the view of the Pakistani fast-food joint, where, thanks to his wild imagination, the gray-bearded villain with a kind look had settled.

Waiting until the end of his broadcast only with difficulty, he hurried to the café. To celebrate this festive occasion, he ordered a glass of wine and put the printed copy of his book on the table. It was an excellent novel, the kind that he never read himself, even at the time when he'd still read novels. He interrupted his reading on the seventy-fifth page, to take a rest and order more wine. The café was crowded tonight because the office upstairs was having a party here. The characters that usually smoked on the balcony on Tuesday were now raising glasses, guffawing, and some even started to dance. He turned his eyes to the joint across the street. Today, for some reason, they were closing sooner than usual; under the half-lowered venetian blinds, he saw how the waitress, now dressed in a black coat, was putting on her backpack. He observed how she fiddled with some mixed-up cords, probably leading from a player, got nervous, stamping her foot in frustration, until from that tiny door a hunched old man with glasses came out and helped her disentangle them. He did it very deftly, showing years-long practice in going over prayer beads. Pity that all this won't fit into the novel, he thought and again immersed himself in the reading. In a few seconds he again raised his head and saw the girl with the backpack walk past him. She went slowly, carrying herself proudly, turned round the glass corner in which he'd settled down, and to his utter astonishment, she entered the café. The bell rang, which nobody except him heard anyway, as the party was in full swing. Unnoticed, the waitress approached the bunch of dancing people and, putting her hand behind her back, she began to feel in the outer pocket of the backpack, where her player must have been lying—cords were leading from there anyway. There was something wrong, he put down his novel, got halfway up from the table and suddenly saw how she, taking out some small device—something like a cell phone or a remote control—pushed a button.

KIRILL KOBRIN writes fiction and nonfiction, co-edits the Moscow magazine of sociology, history, and politics *Neprikosnovenniy Zapas* ("Emergency Rations"), and researches the cultural history of Russia and the Czech Republic. He is the author of fifteen books in Russian, one of them being a tribute to Flann O'Brien, *Tekstoobrabotka* ("Bookhandling"). Critics have hailed him as the "Russian Borges" and one of the founders of Russian psychogeography. His books have been translated into several European languages.

VERONIKA LAKOTOVÁ is a translator of English, Russian and Slovak. She currently lives in Bratislava.

MICHAL AJVAZ, *The Golden Age.*
The Other City.
PIERRE ALBERT-BIROT, *Grabinoulor.*
YUZ ALESHKOVSKY, *Kangaroo.*
FELIPE ALFAU, *Chromos.*
Locos.
IVAN ÂNGELO, *The Celebration.*
The Tower of Glass.
ANTÓNIO LOBO ANTUNES, *Knowledge of Hell.*
The Splendor of Portugal.
SVETISLAV BASARA, *Chinese Letter.*
MIQUEL BAUÇÀ, *The Siege in the Room.*
RENÉ BELLETTO, *Dying.*
MAREK BIEŃCZYK, *Transparency.*
IGNÁCIO DE LOYOLA BRANDÃO,
Anonymous Celebrity.
Zero.
BRIGID BROPHY, *In Transit.*
The Prancing Novelist.
MICHEL BUTOR, *Degrees.*
Mobile.
G. CABRERA INFANTE, *Infante's Inferno.*
Three Trapped Tigers.
JULIETA CAMPOS, *The Fear of Losing Eurydice.*
ANNE CARSON, *Eros the Bittersweet.*
LOUIS-FERDINAND CÉLINE, *North.*
Conversations with Professor Y.
London Bridge.
ERIC CHEVILLARD, *Demolishing Nisard.*
The Author and Me.
MARC CHOLODENKO, *Mordechai Schamz.*
RENÉ CREVEL, *Putting My Foot in It.*
RALPH CUSACK, *Cadenza.*
ARIEL DORFMAN, *Konfidenz.*
COLEMAN DOWELL, *Island People.*
Too Much Flesh and Jabez.
ARKADII DRAGOMOSHCHENKO,
Dust.
WILLIAM EASTLAKE, *The Bamboo Bed.*
Castle Keep.
Lyric of the Circle Heart.

JEAN ECHENOZ, *Chopin's Move.*
STANLEY ELKIN, *A Bad Man.*
Criers and Kibitzers, Kibitzers and Criers.
The Dick Gibson Show.
The Franchiser.
FRANÇOIS EMMANUEL, *Invitation to a Voyage.*
PAUL EMOND, *The Dance of a Sham.*
SALVADOR ESPRIU, *Ariadne in the Grotesque Labyrinth.*
JUAN FILLOY, *Op Oloop.*
GUSTAVE FLAUBERT, *Bouvard and Pécuchet.*
JON FOSSE, *Aliss at the Fire.*
Melancholy.
Melancholy II.
Morning and Evening
MAX FRISCH, *I'm Not Stiller.*
Man in the Holocene.
GÉRARD GAVARRY, *Hoppla! 1 2 3.*
ETIENNE GILSON, *The Arts of the Beautiful.*
Forms and Substances in the Arts.
C. S. GISCOMBE, *Giscome Road.*
Here.
WITOLD GOMBROWICZ, *A Kind of Testament.*
GEORGI GOSPODINOV, *Natural Novel.*
JUAN GOYTISOLO, *Count Julian.*
Juan the Landless.
Makbara.
Marks of Identity.
JIŘÍ GRUŠA, *The Questionnaire.*
MELA HARTWIG, *Am I a Redundant Human Being?*
AIDAN HIGGINS, *Balcony of Europe.*
Blind Man's Bluff.
Bornholm Night-Ferry.
Langrishe, Go Down.
Scenes from a Receding Past.
KEIZO HINO, *Isle of Dreams.*
DRAGO JANČAR, *The Tree with No Name.*
I Saw Her That Night
MIKHEIL JAVAKHISHVILI, *Kvachi.*

FOR A FULL LIST OF PUBLICATIONS, VISIT: www.dalkeyarchive.com

GERT JONKE, *The Distant Sound.*
Homage to Czerny.
The System of Vienna.

JACQUES JOUET, *Mountain R.*
Savage.
Upstaged.

YORAM KANIUK, *Life on Sandpaper.*

ZURAB KARUMIDZE, *Dagny.*

DANILO KIŠ, *The Attic.*
The Lute and the Scars.
Psalm 44.
A Tomb for Boris Davidovich.

ANITA KONKKA, *A Fool's Paradise.*

GEORGE KONRÁD, *The City Builder.*

TADEUSZ KONWICKI, *A Minor Apocalypse.*
The Polish Complex.

ANNA KORDZAIA-SAMADASHVILI,
Me, Margarita.

EMILIO LASCANO TEGUI, *On Elegance While Sleeping.*

ERIC LAURRENT, *Do Not Touch.*

VIOLETTE LEDUC, *La Bâtarde.*

EDOUARD LEVÉ, *Autoportrait.*
Newspaper.
Suicide.
Works.

MARIO LEVI, *Istanbul Was a Fairy Tale.*

JOSÉ LEZAMA LIMA, *Paradiso.*

ROSA LIKSOM, *Dark Paradise.*

OSMAN LINS, *Avalovara.*
The Queen of the Prisons of Greece.

FLORIAN LIPUŠ, *The Errors of Young Tjaž.*

YURI LOTMAN, *Non-Memoirs.*

DAVID MARKSON, *Reader's Block.*
Wittgenstein's Mistress.

CAROLE MASO, *AVA.*

JOSEPH MCELROY, *Night Soul and Other Stories.*

ABDELWAHAB MEDDEB, *Talismano.*

GERHARD MEIER, *Isle of the Dead.*

HERMAN MELVILLE, *The Confidence-Man.*

AMANDA MICHALOPOULOU, *I'd Like.*

CHRISTINE MONTALBETTI, *The Origin of Man.*
Western.

GERALD MURNANE, *Barley Patch.*
Inland.

YVES NAVARRE, *Our Share of Time.*
Sweet Tooth.

ESHKOL NEVO, *Homesick.*

WILFRIDO D. NOLLEDO, *But for the Lovers.*

BORIS A. NOVAK, *The Master of Insomnia.*

FLANN O'BRIEN, *At Swim-Two-Birds.*
The Dalkey Archive.
The Poor Mouth.
The Third Policeman.

CLAUDE OLLIER, *The Mise-en-Scène.*
Wert and the Life Without End.

PATRIK OUŘEDNÍK, *Europeana.*
The Opportune Moment, 1855.

BORIS PAHOR, *Necropolis.*

FERNANDO DEL PASO, *News from the Empire.*
Palinuro of Mexico.

ROBERT PINGET, *Graal Flibuste.*
The Inquisitory.
Mahu or The Material.
Trio.

MANUEL PUIG, *Betrayed by Rita Hayworth.*
The Buenos Aires Affair.
Heartbreak Tango.

RAYMOND QUENEAU, *The Last Days.*
Odile.
Pierrot Mon Ami.
Saint Glinglin.

ANN QUIN, *Berg.*
Passages.
Three.
Tripticks.

ISHMAEL REED, *The Free-Lance Pallbearers.*
The Last Days of Louisiana Red.
Juice!
The Terrible Twos.
Yellow Back Radio Broke-Down.

JASIA REICHARDT, *15 Journeys Warsaw to London.*

RAINER MARIA RILKE, *The Notebooks of Malte Laurids Brigge.*

JULIÁN RÍOS, *The House of Ulysses.*
Larva: A Midsummer Night's Babel.
Poundemonium.

ALAIN ROBBE-GRILLET, *Project for a Revolution in New York.*
A Sentimental Novel.

DANIËL ROBBERECHTS, *Arriving in Avignon.*

JEAN ROLIN, *The Explosion of the Radiator Hose.*

OLIVIER ROLIN, *Hotel Crystal.*

ALIX CLEO ROUBAUD, *Alix's Journal.*

JACQUES ROUBAUD, *The Form of a City Changes Faster, Alas, Than the Human Heart.*
The Great Fire of London.
Hortense in Exile.
Hortense Is Abducted.
Mathematics: The Plurality of Worlds of Lewis.
Some Thing Black.

RAYMOND ROUSSEL, *Impressions of Africa.*

VEDRANA RUDAN, *Night.*

LYDIE SALVAYRE, *The Company of Ghosts.*
The Lecture.
The Power of Flies.

LUIS RAFAEL SÁNCHEZ, *Macho Camacho's Beat.*

NATHALIE SARRAUTE, *Do You Hear Them?*
Martereau.
The Planetarium.

STIG SÆTERBAKKEN, *Siamese.*
Self-Control.
Through the Night.

ARNO SCHMIDT, *Collected Novellas.*
Collected Stories.
Nobodaddy's Children.
Two Novels.

ASAF SCHURR, *Motti.*

VIKTOR SHKLOVSKY, *Bowstring.*
Literature and Cinematography.
Theory of Prose.
Third Factory.
Zoo, or Letters Not about Love.

PIERRE SINIAC, *The Collaborators.*

KJERSTI A. SKOMSVOLD, *The Faster I Walk, the Smaller I Am.*

JOSEF ŠKVORECKÝ, *The Engineer of Human Souls.*

MARKO SOSIČ, *Ballerina, Ballerina.*

ANDRZEJ STASIUK, *Dukla.*
Fado.

LARS SVENDSEN, *A Philosophy of Evil.*

PIOTR SZEWC, *Annihilation.*

GONÇALO M. TAVARES, *A Man: Klaus Klump.*
Jerusalem.
Learning to Pray in the Age of Technique.

LUCIAN DAN TEODOROVICI, *Our Circus Presents...*

NIKANOR TERATOLOGEN, *Assisted Living.*

DUMITRU TSEPENEAG, *Hotel Europa.*
The Necessary Marriage.
Pigeon Post.
Vain Art of the Fugue.

DUBRAVKA UGRESIC, *Lend Me Your Character.*
Thank You for Not Reading.

TOR ULVEN, *Replacement.*

MATI UNT, *Brecht at Night.*
Diary of a Blood Donor.
Things in the Night.

ELOY URROZ, *Friction.*
The Obstacles.

LUISA VALENZUELA, *Dark Desires and the Others.*
He Who Searches.

BORIS VIAN, *Heartsnatcher.*

LLORENÇ VILLALONGA, *The Dolls' Room.*

TOOMAS VINT, *An Unending Landscape.*

ORNELA VORPSI, *The Country Where No One Ever Dies.*

AND MORE...